HENRY C DITZ.

Borzoi Books for Young People

SELECTED BY PHYLLIS R. FENNER

Illustrated by Henry C. Pitz

THERE WAS A HORSE: *Folktales of Many Lands*

GIANTS AND WITCHES: *and a Dragon or Two*

TIME TO LAUGH: *Funny Tales from Here and There*

PRINCESSES AND PEASANT BOYS: *Tales of Enchantment*

ADVENTURE: *Rare and Magical*

Published by Alfred A. Knopf

Demons and Dervishes

TALES WITH "MORE-THAN-ORIENTAL SPLENDOR"

Demons and Dervishes

TALES WITH

More-than-Oriental Splendor

SELECTED BY
Phyllis R. Fenner

ILLUSTRATED BY HENRY C. PITZ

Alfred·A·Knopf
NEW YORK

This is a Borzoi Book, published by
ALFRED A. KNOPF, INC.

Clara's Book

"I stay my haste, I make delays,
For what avails this eager pace?
I stand amid eternal ways
And what is mine
    shall know my face."
—JOHN BURROUGHS

RUBIES *and emeralds. Diamonds and Sapphires. Baskets of them. And some as big as hens' eggs. Goblets, each made from a single ruby, overflowing . . . overflowing with gold pieces. Bolts of precious materials, silks, satins, heavy brocades. Gold dishes to eat upon. Magic lamps. Magic rings. Slaves. Sultans and Tsars. Nightingales and beautiful maidens. Mosques and temples made of white marble, rich with mosaics and crimson hangings. This is Oriental splendor. It is so gorgeous that "no pen can write about it. No tongue can tell it in a tale."*

Demons and djinns to do your bidding . . . at a price. Dervishes and genii. Spirits of the sea, of the mountains, of the land, some good, some evil. Elephants, tigers, jackals, leopards, and fierce eagles. Dragons.

Stories of the East are like light streaming through stained glass windows, reflecting many bits of color.

It is said that thousands of years ago there were "evil spirits and demons as plentiful in the world as wasps in summer," and the good and wise King Solomon got rid of them. Some he conjured into bottles and sank into the depths of the sea. Some he put in boxes and buried in deep forests.

What would you do if you should dig up a box in your garden which said upon it, "Open Not."? Would you, like the little tailor and the soldier's son, open it? Would you like the brave soldier of fortune fight the evil spirits? A King of China once conjured the little demons of the sea into a bottle and buried it in a garden. No one knows where the garden was. Perhaps it was yours. So, watch out. **P. F.**

CONTENTS

Demons and Dervishes

Tales With "More-than-Oriental Splendor"

SIR BUZZ

"OUT STEPPED A LITTLE OLD MAN. HE WAS
ONLY ONE SPAN HIGH, BUT HIS BEARD WAS
A SPAN AND A QUARTER LONG AND TRAILED
UPON THE GROUND."

Once upon a time a soldier died, leaving a widow and one son. They were dreadfully poor, and at last matters became so bad that they had nothing left in the house to eat.

"Mother," said the son, "give me four shillings, and I will go seek my fortune in the wide world."

"Alas!" answered the mother, "and where am I, who haven't a farthing wherewith to buy bread, to find four shillings?"

"There is that old coat of my father's," returned the lad; "look in the pocket—perchance there is something there."

So she looked, and behold! there were six shillings hidden away at the very bottom of the pocket!

"More than I bargained for," quoth the lad, laughing.

"See, mother, these two shillings are for you; you can live on that till I return, the rest will pay my way until I find my fortune."

So he set off to find his fortune, and on the way he saw a tigress, licking her paw, and moaning mournfully. He was just about to run away from the terrible creature, when she called to him faintly, saying, "Good lad, if you will take out this thorn for me, I shall be for ever grateful."

"Not I!" answered the lad. "Why, if I begin to pull it out, and it pains you, you will kill me with a pat of your paw."

"No, no!" cried the tigress, "I will turn my face to this tree, and when the pain comes I will pat *it*."

To this the soldier's son agreed; so he pulled out the thorn, and when the pain came the tigress gave the tree such a blow that the trunk split all to pieces. Then she turned towards the soldier's son, and said gratefully, "Take this box as a reward, my son, but do not open it until you have travelled nine miles."

So the soldier's son thanked the tigress, and set off with the box to find his fortune. Now when he had gone five miles, he felt certain that the box weighed more than it had at first, and every step he took it seemed to grow heavier and heavier. He tried to struggle on—though it was all he could do to carry the box—until he had gone about eight miles and a quarter, when his patience gave way. "I believe that tigress was a witch, and is playing off her tricks upon me," he cried, "but I will stand this nonsense no longer. Lie there, you wretched old box!—heaven knows what is in you, and I don't care."

So saying, he flung the box down on the ground: it burst open with the shock, and out stepped a little old man. He was only one span high, but his beard was a span and a quarter long, and trailed upon the ground.

The little mannikin immediately began to stamp about and scold the lad roundly for letting the box down so violently.

"Upon my word!" quoth the soldier's son, scarcely able to restrain a smile at the ridiculous little figure, "but you are weighty for your size, old gentleman! And what may your name be?"

"Sir Buzz!" snapped the one-span mannikin, still stamping about in a great rage.

"Upon my word!" quoth the soldier's son once more, "if *you* are all the box contained, I am glad I didn't trouble to carry it farther."

"That's not polite," snarled the mannikin; "perhaps if you had carried it the full nine miles you might have found something better; but that's neither here nor there. I'm good enough for you, at any rate, and will serve you faithfully according to my mistress's orders."

"Serve me!—then I wish to goodness you'd serve me with some dinner, for I am mighty hungry! Here are four shillings to pay for it."

No sooner had the soldier's son said this and given the money, than with a *whiz! boom! bing!* like a big bee, Sir Buzz flew through the air to a confectioner's shop in the nearest town. There he stood, the one-span mannikin, with the span and a quarter beard trailing on the ground, just by the big preserving pan, and cried in ever so loud a voice, "Ho! ho! Sir Confectioner, bring me sweets!"

The confectioner looked round the shop, and out of the door, and down the street, but could see no one, for tiny Sir Buzz was quite hidden by the preserving pan. Then the mannikin called out louder still, "Ho! ho! Sir

Confectioner, bring me sweets!" And when the confectioner looked in vain for his customer, Sir Buzz grew
angry, and ran and pinched him on the legs, and kicked
him on the foot, saying, "Impudent knave! do you mean
to say you can't see *me*? Why, I was standing by the preserving pan all the time!"

The confectioner apologized humbly, and hurried
away to bring out his best sweets for his irritable little
customer. Then Sir Buzz chose about a hundredweight of
them, and said, "Quick, tie them up in something and
give them into my hand; I'll carry them home."

"They will be a good weight, sir," smiled the confectioner.

"What business is that of yours, I should like to know?"
snapped Sir Buzz. "Just you do as you're told, and here is
your money." So saying, he jingled the four shillings in
his pocket.

"As you please, sir," replied the man cheerfully, as he
tied up the sweets into a huge bundle and placed it on the
little mannikin's outstretched hand, fully expecting him
to sink under the weight; when lo! with a *boom! bing!*
he whizzed off with the money still in his pocket.

He alighted at a corn-chandler's shop, and, standing
behind a basket of flour, called out at the top of his voice,
"Ho! ho! Sir Chandler, bring me flour!"

And when the corn-chandler looked round the shop,
and out of the window, and down the street, without
seeing anybody, the one-span mannikin, with his beard
trailing on the ground, cried again louder than before,
"Ho! ho! Sir Chandler, bring me flour!"

Then on receiving no answer, he flew into a violent
rage, and ran and bit the unfortunate corn-chandler on
the leg, pinched him, and kicked him, saying, "Impudent

varlet! Don't pretend you couldn't see *me*! Why, I was standing close beside you behind that basket!"

So the corn-chandler apologized humbly for his mistake, and asked Sir Buzz how much flour he wanted.

"Two hundredweight," replied the mannikin. "Two hundredweight, neither more nor less. Tie it up in a bundle, and I'll take it with me."

"Your honor has a cart or beast of burden with you, doubtless?" said the chandler, "for two hundredweight is a heavy load."

"What's that to you?" shrieked Sir Buzz, stamping his foot. "Isn't it enough if I pay for it?" And then he jingled the money in his pocket again.

So the corn-chandler tied up the flour in a bundle, and placed it in the mannikin's outstretched hand, fully expecting it would crush him, when, with a whiz! Sir Buzz flew off, with the shillings still in his pocket. *Boom! bing! boom!*

The soldier's son was just wondering what had become of his one-span servant, when, with a whir! the little fellow alighted beside him, and wiping his face with his handkerchief, as if he were dreadfully hot and tired, said thoughtfully, "Now I do hope I've brought enough, but you men have such terrible appetites!"

"More than enough, I should say," laughed the lad, looking at the huge bundles.

Then Sir Buzz cooked the griddle-cakes, and the soldier's son ate three of them and a handful of sweets; but the one-span mannikin gobbled up all the rest, saying at each mouthful, "You men have such terrible appetites—such terrible appetites!"

After that, the soldier's son and his servant Sir Buzz travelled ever so far, until they came to the King's city.

Now the King had a daughter called Princess Blossom, who was so lovely, and tender, and slim, and fair, that she only weighed five flowers. Every morning she was weighed in golden scales, and the scale always turned when the fifth flower was put in, neither less nor more.

Now it so happened that the soldier's son by chance caught a glimpse of the lovely, tender, slim, and fair Princess Blossom, and, of course, he fell desperately in love with her. He would neither sleep nor eat his dinner, and did nothing all day long but say to his faithful mannikin, "Oh, dearest Sir Buzz! Oh, kind Sir Buzz!—carry me to the Princess Blossom, that I may see and speak to her."

"Carry you!" snapped the little fellow scornfully, "that's a likely story! Why, you're ten times as big as I am. You should carry *me*!"

Nevertheless, when the soldier's son begged and prayed, growing pale and pining away with thinking of the Princess Blossom, Sir Buzz, who had a kind heart, was moved, and bade the lad sit on his hand. Then with a tremendous *boom! bing! boom!* they whizzed away and were in the palace in a second. Being night-time, the Princess was asleep; nevertheless the booming wakened her and she was quite frightened to see a handsome young man kneeling beside her. She began of course to scream, but stopped at once when the soldier's son with the greatest politeness, and in the most elegant of language, begged her not to be alarmed. And after that they talked together about everything delightful, while Sir Buzz stood at the door and did sentry; but he stood a brick up on end first, so that he might not seem to pry upon the young people.

Now when the dawn was just breaking, the soldier's son and Princess Blossom, wearied of talking, fell asleep;

whereupon Sir Buzz, being a faithful servant, said to himself, "Now what is to be done? If my master remains here asleep, some one will discover him, and he will be killed as sure as my name is Buzz; but if I wake him, ten to one he will refuse to go."

So without more ado he put his hand under the bed, and *bing! boom!* carried it into a large garden outside the town. There he set it down in the shade of the biggest tree, and pulling up the next biggest one by the roots, threw it over his shoulder, and marched up and down keeping guard.

Before long the whole town was in a commotion, because the Princess Blossom had been carried off, and all the world and his wife turned out to look for her. By and by the one-eyed Chief Constable came to the garden gate.

"What do you want here?" cried valiant Sir Buzz, making passes at him with the tree.

The Chief Constable with his one eye could see nothing save the branches, but he replied sturdily, "I want the Princess Blossom!"

"I'll blossom you! Get out of *my* garden, will you?" shrieked the one-span mannikin, with his one and quarter span beard trailing on the ground; and with that he belabored the Constable's pony so hard with the tree that it bolted away, nearly throwing its rider.

The poor man went straight to the King, saying, "Your Majesty! I am convinced your Majesty's daughter, the Princess Blossom, is in your Majesty's garden, just outside the town, as there is a tree there which fights terribly."

Upon this the King summoned all his horses and men, and going to the garden tried to get in; but Sir Buzz behind the tree routed them all, for half were killed, and the rest ran away. The noise of the battle, however, awoke the young couple, and as they were now convinced they could no longer exist apart, they determined to fly together. So when the fight was over, the soldier's son, the Princess Blossom, and Sir Buzz set out to see the world.

Now the soldier's son was so enchanted with his good luck in winning the Princess, that he said to Sir Buzz, "My fortune is made already; so I shan't want you any more, and you can go back to your mistress."

"Pooh!" said Sir Buzz. "Young people always think so; however, have it your own way, only take this hair out of my beard, and if you *should* get into trouble, just burn it in the fire. I'll come to your aid."

So Sir Buzz boomed off, and the soldier's son and the Princess Blossom lived and travelled together very happily, until at last they lost their way in a forest, and wandered about for some time without any food. When they were nearly starving, a Brahman found them, and hearing their story said, "Alas! you poor children!—come home with me, and I will give you something to eat."

Now had he said "I will eat you," it would have been much nearer the mark, for he was no Brahman, but a dreadful vampire, who loved to devour handsome young men and slender girls. But, knowing nothing of all this, the couple went home with him quite cheerfully. He was most polite, and when they arrived at his house, said, "Please get ready whatever you want to eat, for I have no cook. Here are my keys; open all my cupboards save the one with the golden key. Meanwhile I will go and gather firewood."

Then the Princess Blossom began to prepare the food, while the soldier's son opened all the cupboards. In them he saw lovely jewels, and dresses, and cups and platters, such bags of gold and silver, that his curiosity got the better of his discretion, and, regardless of the Brahman's warning, he said, "I *will* see what wonderful thing is hidden in the cupboard with the golden key." So he opened it, and lo! it was full of human skulls, picked quite clean, and beautifully polished. At this dreadful sight the soldier's son flew back to the Princess Blossom, and said, "We are lost! we are lost!—this is no Brahman, but a horrid vampire!"

At that moment they heard him at the door, and the Princess, who was very brave and kept her wits about her, had barely time to thrust the magic hair into the fire, before the vampire, with sharp teeth and fierce eyes, appeared. But at the selfsame moment a *boom! boom! binging* noise was heard in the air, coming nearer and nearer. Whereupon the vampire who knew very well who his enemy was, changed into a heavy rain pouring down in torrents, hoping thus to drown Sir Buzz, but *he* changed into the storm wind beating back the rain. Then the vampire changed to a dove, but Sir Buzz, pursuing it as a hawk, pressed it so hard that it had barely time to change into a rose, and drop into King Indra's lap as he sat in his celestial court listening to the singing of some dancing girls. Then Sir Buzz, quick as thought, changed into an old musician, and standing beside the bard who was thrumming the guitar, said, "Brother, you are tired; let *me* play."

And he played so wonderfully, and sang with such piercing sweetness, that King Indra said, "What shall I give you as a reward? Name what you please and it shall be yours."

Then Sir Buzz said, "I only ask the rose that is in your Majesty's lap."

"I had rather you asked more, or less," replied King Indra; "it is but a rose, yet it fell from heaven; nevertheless it is yours."

So saying, he threw the rose towards the musician, and lo! the petals fell in a shower on the ground. Sir Buzz went down on his knees and instantly gathered them up; but one petal escaping, changed into a mouse. Whereupon Sir Buzz, with the speed of lightning, turned into a cat, which caught and gobbled up the mouse.

Now all this time the Princess Blossom and the soldier's son, shivering and shaking, were awaiting the issue of the combat in the vampire's hut; when suddenly, with a *bing! boom!* Sir Buzz arrived victorious, shook his head, and said, "You two had better go home, for you are not fit to take care of yourselves."

Then he gathered together all the jewels and gold in one hand, placed the Princess and the soldier's son in the other, and whizzed away home, to where the poor mother —who all this time had been living on the two shillings— was delighted to see them.

Then with a louder *boom! bing! boom!* than usual, Sir Buzz, without even waiting for thanks, whizzed out of sight, and was never seen or heard of again.

But the soldier's son and the Princess Blossom lived happily ever after.

2

WOMAN'S WIT

<><><><><><><><><><><><><><><><><><><><><><><><><><><><><><><><><><><><><>

"WHEN MAN'S STRENGTH FAILS, WOMAN'S WIT PREVAILS."

<><><><><><><><><><><><><><><><><><><><><><><><><><><><><><><><><><><><><>

In the days when the great and wise King Solomon lived and ruled, evil spirits and demons were as plentiful in the world as wasps in summer.

So King Solomon, who was so wise and knew so many potent spells that he had power over evil such as no man has had before or since, set himself to work to put those enemies of mankind out of the way. Some he conjured into bottles, and sank into the depths of the sea; some he buried in the earth; some he destroyed altogether, as one burns hair in a candle-flame.

Now, one pleasant day when King Solomon was walking in his garden with his hands behind his back, and his thoughts busy as bees with this or that, he came face to face with a Demon, who was a prince of his kind. "Ho, little man!" cried the evil spirit, in a loud voice, "art not thou the wise King Solomon who conjures my brethren into brass chests and glass bottles? Come, try a fall at wrestling with me, and whoever conquers shall be master

[15]

over the other for all time. What do you say to such an offer as that?"

"I say aye!" said King Solomon, and, without another word, he stripped off his royal robes and stood bare breasted, man to man with the other.

The world never saw the like of that wrestling-match betwixt the king and the Demon, for they struggled and strove together from the seventh hour in the morning to the sunset in the evening, and during that time the sky was clouded over as black as night, and the lightning forked and shot, and the thunder roared and bellowed, and the earth shook and quaked.

But at last the king gave the enemy an under twist, and flung him down on the earth so hard that the apples fell from the trees; and then, panting and straining, he held the evil one down, knee on neck. Thereupon the sky presently cleared again, and all was as pleasant as a spring day.

King Solomon bound the Demon with spells, and made him serve him for seven years. First, he had him build a splendid palace, the like of which was not to be seen within the bounds of the seven rivers; then he made him set around the palace a garden, such as I for one wish I may see some time or other. Then, when the Demon had done all that the king wished, the king conjured him into a bottle, corked it tightly, and set the royal seal on the stopper. Then he took the bottle a thousand miles away into the wilderness, and, when no man was looking, buried it in the ground, and this is the way the story begins.

Well, the years came and the years went, and the world grew older and older, and kept changing (as all things

do but two), so that by-and-by the wilderness where
King Solomon had hid the bottle became a great town,
with people coming and going, and all as busy as bees
about their own business and other folk's affairs.

Among these townspeople was a little Tailor, who
made clothes for many a worse man to wear, and who
lived all alone in a little house with no one to darn his
stockings for him, and no one to meddle with his coming
and going, for he was a bachelor.

The little Tailor was a thrifty soul, and by hook and
crook had laid by enough money to fill a small pot, and
then he had to bethink himself of some safe place to hide
it. So one night he took a spade and a lamp and went out
in the garden to bury his money. He drove his spade
into the ground—and click! He struck something hard
that rang under his foot with a sound as of iron. "Hello!"
said he, "what have we here?" and if he had known as
much as you and I do, he would have filled in the earth,
and tramped it down, and have left that plate of broth
for somebody else to burn his mouth with.

As it was, he scraped away the soil, and then he found
a box of adamant, with a ring in the lid to lift it by. The
Tailor clutched the ring and bent his back, and up came
the box with the damp earth sticking to it. He cleaned the
mould away, and there he saw, written in red letters,
these words:

"Open Not."

You may be sure that after he had read these words he
was not long in breaking open the lid of the box with his
spade.

Inside the first box he found a second, and upon it the
same words:

"*Open not.*"

Within the second box was another, and within that still another, until there were seven in all, and on each was written the same words:

"*Open not.*"

Inside the seventh box was a roll of linen, and inside that a bottle filled with nothing but blue smoke; and I wish that bottle had burned the Tailor's fingers when he touched it.

"And is this all?" said the little Tailor, turning the bottle upside down and shaking it, and peeping at it by the light of the lamp. "Well, since I have gone so far I might as well open it, as I have already opened the seven boxes." Thereupon he broke the seal that stoppered it.

Pop! Out flew the cork, and— Puff! Out came the smoke; not all at once, but in a long thread that rose up as high as the stars, and then spread until it hid their light.

The Tailor stared and goggled and gaped to see so much smoke come out of such a little bottle, and, as he goggled and stared, the smoke began to gather together again, thicker and thicker, and darker and darker, until it was as black as ink. Then out from it there stepped one with eyes that shone like sparks of fire, and who had a countenance so terrible that the Tailor's skin quivered and shrivelled, and his tongue clove to the roof of his mouth at the sight of it.

"Who art thou?" said the terrible being, in a voice that made the very marrow of the poor Tailor's bones turn soft from terror.

"If you please, sir," said he, "I am only a little tailor."

The evil being lifted up both hands and eyes. "How wonderful," he cried, "that one little tailor can undo in a moment that which took the wise Solomon a whole day to accomplish, and in the doing of which he well-nigh broke the sinews of his heart!" Then, turning to the Tailor, who stood trembling like a rabbit, "Hark thee!" said he. "For two thousand years I lay there in that bottle, and no one came nigh to aid me. Thou hast liberated me, and thou shalt not go unrewarded. Every morning at the seventh hour I will come to thee, and I will perform for thee whatever task thou mayest command me. But there is one condition attached to the agreement, and woe be to thee if that condition is broken. If any morning I should come to thee, and thou hast no task for me to do, I shall wring thy neck as thou mightest wring the neck of a sparrow." Thereupon he was gone in an instant, leaving the little Tailor half dead with terror.

Now it happened that the prime-minister of that country had left an order with the Tailor for a suit of clothes, so the next morning, when the Demon came, the little man set him to work on the bench, with his legs tucked up like a journeyman tailor. "I want," said he, "such and such a suit of clothes."

"You shall have them," said the Demon; and thereupon he began snipping in the air, and cutting most wonderful patterns of silks and satins out of nothing at all, and the little Tailor sat and gaped and stared. Then the Demon began to drive the needle like a spark of fire—the like was never seen in all the seven kingdoms, for the clothes seemed to make themselves.

At last, at the end of a little while, the Demon stood up and brushed his hands. "They are done," said he, and thereupon he instantly vanished. But the Tailor cared

little for that, for upon the bench there lay such a suit of
clothes of silk and satin stuff, sewed with threads of gold
and silver and set with jewels, as the eyes of man never
saw before; and the Tailor packed them up and marched
off with them himself to the prime-minister.

The prime-minister wore the clothes to court that very
day, and before evening they were the talk of the town.
All the world ran to the Tailor and ordered clothes of
him, and his fortune was made. Every day the Demon
created new suits of clothes out of nothing at all, so that
the Tailor grew rich, and held his head up in the world.

As time went along he laid heavier and heavier tasks

upon the Demon s back, and demanded of him more and more; but all the while the Demon kept his own counsel, and said never a word.

One morning, as the Tailor sat in his shop window taking the world easy—for he had little or nothing to do now —he heard a great hubbub in the street below, and when he looked down he saw that it was the king's daughter passing by. It was the first time that the Tailor had seen her, and when he saw her his heart stood still within him, and then began fluttering like a little bird, for one so beautiful was not to be met with in the four corners of the world. Then she was gone.

All that day the little Tailor could do nothing but sit and think of the princess, and the next morning when the Demon came he was thinking of her still.

"What hast thou for me to do to-day?" said the Demon, as he always said of a morning.

The little Tailor was waiting for the question.

"I would like you," said he, "to send to the king's palace, and to ask him to let me have his daughter for my wife."

"Thou shalt have thy desire," said the Demon. Thereupon he smote his hands together like a clap of thunder, and instantly the walls of the room clove asunder, and there came out four-and-twenty handsome youths, clad in cloth of gold and silver. After these four-and-twenty there came another one who was the chief of them all, and before whom, splendid as they were, the four-and-twenty paled like stars in daylight. "Go to the king's palace," said the Demon to that one, "and deliver this message: The Tailor of Tailors, the Master of Masters, and One Greater than a King asks for his daughter to wife."

"To hear is to obey," said the other, and bowed his forehead to the earth.

Never was there such a hubbub in the town as when those five-and-twenty, in their clothes of silver and gold, rode through the streets to the king's palace. As they came near, the gates of the palace flew open before them, and the king himself came out to meet them. The leader of the five-and-twenty leaped from his horse, and, kissing the ground before the king, delivered his message: "The Tailor of Tailors, the Master of Masters, and One Greater than a King asks for thy daughter to wife."

When the king heard what the messenger said, he thought and pondered a long time. At last he said, "If he who sent you is the Master of Masters, and greater than a king, let him send me an asking gift such as no king could send."

"It shall be as you desire," said the messenger, and thereupon the five-and-twenty rode away as they had come, followed by crowds of people.

The next morning when the Demon came the tailor was ready and waiting for him. "What hast thou for me to do to-day?" said the Evil One.

"I want," said the tailor, "a gift to send to the king such as no other king could send him."

"Thou shalt have thy desire," said the Demon. Thereupon he smote his hands together, and summoned, not five-and-twenty young men, but fifty youths, all clad in clothes more splendid than the others.

All of the fifty sat upon coal-black horses, with saddles of silver and housings of silk and velvet embroidered with gold. In the midst of all the five-and-seventy there rode a youth in cloth of silver embroidered in pearls. In his hand he bore something wrapped in a white napkin, and that was the present for the king such as no other king could give. So said the Demon: "Take it to the royal palace, and tell his majesty that it is from the Tailor of Tailors, the Master of Masters, and One Greater than a King."

"To hear is to obey," said the young man, and then they all rode away.

When they came to the palace the gates flew open before them, and the king came out to meet them. The young man who bore the present dismounted and prostrated himself in the dust, and, when the king bade him arise, he unwrapped the napkin, and gave to the king a goblet made of one single ruby, and filled to the brim with pieces of gold. Moreover, the cup was of such a kind that whenever it was emptied of its money it instantly became full again. "The Tailor of Tailors, and Master of Masters, and One Greater than a King sends your majesty this goblet, and bids me, his ambassador, to ask for your daughter," said the young man.

When the king saw what had been sent him he was filled with amazement. "Surely," said he to himself, "there can be no end to the power of one who can give such a gift as this." Then to the messenger, "Tell your master that he shall have my daughter for his wife if he will build over yonder a palace such as no man ever saw or no king ever lived in before."

"It shall be done," said the young man, and then they all went away, as the others had done the day before.

The next morning when the Demon appeared the Tailor was ready for him. "Build me," said he, "such and such a palace in such and such a place."

And the Demon said, "It shall be done." He smote his hands together, and instantly there came a cloud of mist that covered and hid the spot where the palace was to be built. Out from the cloud there came such a banging and hammering and clapping and clattering as the people of that town never heard before. Then when evening had come the cloud arose, and there, where the king had pointed out, stood a splendid palace as white as snow, with roofs and domes of gold and silver. As the king stood looking and wondering at this sight, there came five hundred young men riding, and one in the midst of all who wore a golden crown on his head, and upon his body a long robe stiff with diamonds and pearls. "We come," said he, "from the Tailor of Tailors, and Master of Masters, and One Greater than a King, to ask you to let him have your daughter for his wife."

"Tell him to come!" cried the king, in admiration, "for the princess is his."

The next morning when the Demon came he found the Tailor dancing and shouting for joy. "The princess is mine!" he cried, "so make me ready for her."

"It shall be done," said the Demon, and thereupon he began to make the Tailor ready for his wedding. He brought him to a marble bath of water, in which he washed away all that was coarse and ugly, and from which the little man came forth as beautiful as the sun. Then the Demon clad him in the finest linen, and covered him with clothes such as even the emperor of India never wore. Then he smote his hands together, and the wall of the tailor-shop opened as it had done twice before, and there came forth forty slaves clad in crimson, and bearing bowls full of money in their hands. After them came two leading a horse as white as snow, with a saddle of gold studded with diamonds and rubies and emeralds and sapphires. After came a body-guard of

twenty warriors clad in gold armor. Then the Tailor
mounted his horse and rode away to the king's palace,
and as he rode the slaves scattered the money amongst
the crowd, who scrambled for it and cheered the Tailor
to the skies.

That night the princess and the Tailor were married,
and all the town was lit with bonfires and fireworks. The
two rode away in the midst of a great crowd of nobles
and courtiers to the palace which the Demon had built
for the Tailor; and, as the princess gazed upon him, she
thought that she had never beheld so noble and handsome a man as her husband. So she and the Tailor were
the happiest couple in the world.

But the next morning the Demon appeared as he had
appeared ever since the Tailor had let him out of the
bottle, only now he grinned till his teeth shone and his
face turned black. "What hast thou for me to do?" said
he, and at the words the Tailor's heart began to quake,
for he remembered what was to happen to him when he
could find the Demon no more work to do—that his neck
was to be wrung—and now he began to see that he had
all that he could ask for in the world. Yes; what was there
to ask for now?

"I have nothing more for you to do," said he to the
Demon; "you have done all that man could ask—you may
go now."

"Go!" cried the Demon, "I shall not go until I have
done all that I have to do. Give me work, or I shall wring
your neck." And his fingers began to twitch.

Then the Tailor began to see into what a net he had
fallen. He began to tremble like one in an ague. He
turned his eyes up and down, for he did not know where

to look for aid. Suddenly, as he looked out of the window, a thought struck him. "Maybe," thought he, "I can give the Demon such a task that even he cannot do it." "Yes, yes!" he cried. "I have thought of something for you to do. Make me out yonder in front of my palace a lake of water a mile long and a mile wide, and let it be lined throughout with white marble, and filled with water as clear as crystal."

"It shall be done," said the Demon. As he spoke he spat in the air, and instantly a thick fog arose from the earth and hid everything from sight. Then presently from the midst of the fog there came a great noise of chipping and hammering, of digging and delving, of rushing and gurgling. All day the noise and the fog continued, and then at sunset the one ceased and the other cleared away. The poor Tailor looked out the window, and when he saw what he saw his teeth chattered in his head, for there was a lake a mile long and a mile broad, lined within with white marble, and filled with water as clear as crystal, and he knew that the Demon would come the next morning for another task to do.

That night he slept little or none, and when the seventh hour of the morning came the castle began to rock and tremble, and there stood the Demon, and his hair bristled and his eyes shone like sparks of fire. "What hast thou for me to do?" said he, and the poor Tailor could do nothing but look at him with a face as white as dough.

"What hast thou for me to do?" said the Demon again, and then at last the Tailor found his wits and his tongue from sheer terror. "Look!" said he, "at the great mountain over yonder; remove it, and make in its place a level plain with fields and orchards and gardens." And he thought to himself when he had spoken, "Surely, even the Demon cannot do that."

"It shall be done," said the Demon, and, so saying, he stamped his heel upon the ground. Instantly the earth began to tremble and quake, and there came a great rumbling like the sound of thunder. A cloud of darkness gathered in the sky, until at last all was as black as the blackest midnight. Then came a roaring and a cracking and a crashing, such as man never heard before. All day it continued, until the time of the setting of the sun, when suddenly the uproar ceased, and the darkness cleared away; and when the Tailor looked out of the window the mountain was gone, and in its place were fields and orchards and gardens.

It was very beautiful to see, but when the Tailor beheld it his knees began to smite together, and the sweat ran down his face in streams. All that night he walked up and down and up and down, but he could not think of one other task for the Demon to do.

When the next morning came the Demon appeared like a whirlwind. His face was as black as ink and smoke, and sparks of fire flew from his nostrils.

"What have you for me to do?" cried he.

"I have nothing for you to do!" piped the poor Tailor.

"Nothing?" cried the Demon.

"Nothing."

"Then prepare to die."

"Stop!" said the Tailor, falling on his knees, "let me first see my wife."

"So be it," said the Demon, and if he had been wiser he would have said "No."

When the Tailor came to the princess, he flung himself on his face, and began to weep and wail. The princess asked him what was the matter, and at last, by dint of question, got the story from him, piece by piece. When she had it all she began laughing. "Why did you not come to me before?" said she, "instead of making all this trouble and uproar for nothing at all? I will give the Monster a task to do." She plucked a single curling hair from her head. "Here," said she, "let him take this hair and make it straight."

The Tailor was full of doubt; nevertheless, as there was nothing better to do, he took it to the Demon.

"Hast thou found me a task to do?" cried the Demon.

"Yes," said the Tailor. "It is only a little thing. Here is a hair from my wife's head; take it and make it straight."

When the Demon heard what was the task that the Tailor had set him to do he laughed aloud; but that was because he did not know. He took the hair and stroked it between his thumb and finger, and, when he had done, it curled more than ever. Then he looked serious, and slapped it between his palms, and that did not better matters, for it curled as much as ever. Then he frowned, and began beating the hair with his palm upon his knees, and that only made it worse. All that day he labored and strove át his task trying to make that one little hair straight, and, when the sun set, there was the hair just as crooked as ever. Then, as the great round sun sank red behind the trees, the Demon knew that he was beaten. "I am conquered! I am conquered!" he howled, and flew away, bellowing so dreadfully that all the world trembled.

So ends the story, with only this to say:

Where man's strength fails, woman's wit prevails.

For, to my mind, the princess—not to speak of her husband the little Tailor—did more with a single little hair and her mother wit than King Solomon with all his wisdom.

3

THE PHANTOM CATS

"WHISPER NOT TO SHIPPEITARO THAT THE
PHANTOM CATS ARE NEAR, WHISPER NOT TO
SHIPPEITARO LEST HE SOON APPEAR."

A ruined temple stood in a lonely wood. All about
it was a trackless forest. The huge trees waved above it,
the leaves in the thicket whispered about it, the sun
goddess seldom shone upon it with her light.

Uguisu,[1] poet of the woods, sang in the plum tree near
by. He sang the poet's song to the plum tree which he
loved:

"Send forth your fragrance upon the eastern winds,
Oh flower of the plum tree,
Forget not the spring because of the absence of the sun."

Ruined though the temple was, it still held a shrine
and hither came Wakiki Mononofu, a young Samurai.[2]
He was a brave young soldier who was seeking his fortune in the wide, wide world. He had lost his way and
wandered in the forest seeking the path, until at length

[1] The nightingale.　　　　[2] *Samurai,* a man of the military class.

he came to the little clear space where was the temple. A storm was coming up, and a palace could not have seemed more welcome to the young warrior.

"Here is all I want," he said to himself. "Here I shall have a shelter from the storm god's wrath, and a place to sleep and dream of glory and adventure. What more could be desired?"

Then he wrapped himself in his mantle, curled up in a corner of the sacred room, and soon fell asleep. But his slumber did not last long. His pleasant dreams were disturbed by horrid sounds, and waking, he sprang to his feet and looked out of the temple door.

There he saw a troop of monstrous cats which seemed in the weird moonlight like phantoms, marching across the clear space in front of the temple, and dancing a wild dance. As they danced they uttered horrid sounds, yells, and wicked laughs; and through these he could hear the words of a strange chant:

> "Whisper not to Shippeitaro
> That the Phantom Cats are near,
> Whisper not to Shippeitaro
> Lest he soon appear."

Wakiki crouched low behind the door; for, brave as he was, there was something so dreadful in the appearance of the creatures that he did not want them to see him. Soon, however, with a chorus of wild yells, they disappeared as quickly as they had come. Then Wakiki lay down and slept again, nor did he waken until the sun goddess peered into the temple and whispered to him that it was morning.

By the morning light it was easy to find the path which the night's shadows had hidden from him, and being very hungry he started out to seek some dwelling. The path led away from the temple, in an opposite direction to that from which he had come the night before. Soon, however, he came out of the forest and saw a little hamlet surrounded by green fields.

"How fortunate I am," he cried joyfully. "Here are houses, and so there must be people, and people must have something to eat. If they are kind they will share with me, and I am starving for a bowl of rice."

He hurried to the nearest cottage, but as he approached he heard sounds of bitter weeping. He went

up to the door, and was met by a sweet young girl whose eyes were red with crying. She greeted him kindly, and he asked her for food.

"Enter and welcome," said she. "My parents are about to be served with breakfast. You shall join them, for no one must pass our door hungry."

Thanking her the young warrior went in and seated himself upon the floor. The parents of the young girl greeted him courteously. A small table was set before him, and on it was placed rice and tea. He ate heartily, and, when he had finished eating, rose to go.

"Thank you very many times for such a good meal, kind friends," he said.

"You have been welcome. Go in peace," said the master of the house.

"And may happiness be yours," returned the young Samurai.

"Happiness can never again be ours," said the old man, with a sad face, as his daughter left the room. Her mother followed her and from behind the paper partitions of the breakfast room, Wakiki could hear sounds as if she were trying to comfort the young girl.

"You are then in trouble?" he asked, not liking to be inquisitive, and yet wishing to show sympathy.

"Terrible trouble," said the father. "There is no help! Know, gentle Samurai, that there is within the forest a ruined temple. This shrine, once the home of sacred things, is now the abode of horrors too terrible for words. Each year a mountain spirit, a demon whom no one has ever seen, demands from us a victim, upon pain of destroying the whole village. The victim is placed in a cage and carried to the temple just at sunset. There she is left and no one knows what is her fate, for in the morning not a trace of her remains. It must always be the fairest maiden of the village who is offered up and this year, alas, it is my daughter's turn;" and the old man buried his face in his hands and groaned.

"I should think this strange thing would make the young girls of your village far from vain and each would wish to be the ugliest," said the young warrior. "It is terrible indeed, but do not despair. I am sure I shall find a way to help you." He paused to think. "Tell me, who is Shippeitaro?" he asked suddenly, as he remembered the scene of the night before.

"Shippeitaro is a beautiful dog owned by our lord the prince," said the old man, wondering at the question.

"That will be just the thing," cried the Samurai. "Keep your daughter closely at home. Do not allow her out of your sight. Trust me and she shall be saved."

He hurried away, and having found the castle of the prince, he begged that just for one night Shippeitaro be lent to him.

"Upon condition that you bring him back to me safe and sound," said the prince.

"To-morrow he shall return in safety," the young warrior promised.

Taking Shippeitaro with him he returned to the village; and when evening came, he placed the dog in the cage which was to have carried the maiden.

"Take him to the ruined temple," he said to the bearers, and they obeyed.

When they reached the little shrine they placed the cage on the ground and ran away to the village as fast as their legs could carry them. The young warrior laughed softly, saying to himself, "For once fear is greater than curiosity."

He hid himself in the little temple as before, and so quiet was the spot that he could scarcely keep awake. Soon he was aroused, however, by the same weird chant he had heard the evening before. Through the darkness came the same troop of fearful phantom cats led by a fierce Tom cat, the largest he had ever seen. As they came, they chanted with unearthly screeches,

> "Whisper not to Shippeitaro,
> That the Phantom Cats are near,
> Whisper not to Shippeitaro
> Lest he soon appear."

The song was scarcely ended, when the great Tom cat caught sight of the cage and sprang upon it with a fierce yowl. With one sweep of his paw he tore open the lid, when instead of the dainty morsel he had expected, out leaped Shippeitaro! The noble dog sprang upon the beast and shook him as a cat shakes a rat, while the other beasts stood still in amazement. Drawing his sword the young warrior dashed to Shippeitaro's aid and to such good purpose that in a few moments the phantom cats were no more.

"Brave dog!" cried Wakiki. "You have delivered a whole village by your courage! Let us return and tell the people what has happened, that all men may do you honor."

Patting the dog on the head he led him back to the village. There in terror the maiden awaited his return, but great was her joy when she heard of her deliverance.

"Oh, sir," she cried. "I can never thank you! I am the only child of my parents, and no one would have been left to care for them had I gone to be the monster's victim!"

"Do not thank me," said the young warrior. "I have done little. All the thanks of the village are due to the brave Shippeitaro. It was he who destroyed the phantom cats."

4

THE STORY OF THE SEVEN SIMONS

"THEY WORE RED SHIRTS BOUND WITH GOLD
BRAID, AND WERE SO MUCH ALIKE THAT ONE
COULD HARDLY TELL ONE FROM ANOTHER."

Far, far away, beyond all sorts of countries, seas, and rivers, there stood a splendid city where lived King Archidej, who was as good as he was rich and handsome. His great army was made up of men ready to obey his slightest wish; he owned forty times forty cities, and in each city he had ten palaces with silver doors, golden roofs, and crystal windows. His council consisted of the twelve wisest men in the country, whose long beards flowed down over their breasts, each of whom was as learned as a whole college. This council always told the king the exact truth.

Now the king had everything to make him happy, but he did not enjoy anything because he could not find a bride to his mind.

One day, as he sat in his palace looking out to sea, a

great ship sailed into the harbor and several merchants came on shore. Said the king to himself: "These people have travelled far and beheld many lands. I will ask them if they have seen any princess who is as clever and as handsome as I am."

So he ordered the merchants to be brought before him, and when they came he said: "You have travelled much and visited many wonders. I wish to ask you a question, and I beg you to answer truthfully.

"Have you anywhere seen or heard of the daughter of an emperor, king, or a prince, who is as clever and as handsome as I am, and who would be worthy to be my wife and the queen of my country?"

The merchants considered for some time. At last the eldest of them said: "I have heard that across many seas, in the Island of Busan, there is a mighty king, whose daughter, the Princess Helena, is so lovely that she can certainly not be plainer than your Majesty, and so clever that the wisest greybeard cannot guess her riddles."

"Is the island far off, and which is the way to it?"

"It is not near," was the answer. "The journey would take ten years, and we do not know the way. And even if we did, what use would that be? The princess is no bride for you."

"How dare you say so?" cried the king angrily.

"Your Majesty must pardon us; but just think for a moment. Should you send an envoy to the island he will take ten years to get there and ten more to return— twenty years in all. Will not the princess have grown old in that time and have lost all her beauty?"

The king reflected gravely. Then he thanked the merchants, gave them leave to trade in his country without paying any duties, and dismissed them.

After they were gone the king remained deep in thought. He felt puzzled and anxious; so he decided to ride into the country to distract his mind, and sent for his huntsmen and falconers. The huntsmen blew their horns, the falconers took their hawks on their wrists, and off they all set out across country till they came to a green hedge. On the other side of the hedge stretched a great field of maize as far as the eye could reach, and the yellow ears swayed to and fro in the gentle breeze like a rippling sea of gold.

The king drew rein and admired the field. "Upon my word," said he, "whoever dug and planted it must be good workmen. If all the fields in my kingdom were as well cared for as this, there would be more bread than my people could eat." And he wished to know to whom the field belonged.

Off rushed all his followers at once to do his bidding, and found a nice, tidy farmhouse, in front of which sat seven peasants, lunching on rye bread and drinking water. They wore red shirts bound with gold braid, and were so much alike that one could hardly tell one from another.

The messengers asked: "Who owns this field of golden maize?" And the seven brothers answered: "The field is ours."

"And who are you?"

"We are King Archidej's laborers."

These answers were repeated to the king, who ordered the brothers to be brought before him at once. On being asked who they were, the eldest said, bowing low:

"We, King Archidej, are your laborers, children of one father and mother, and we all have the same name, for each of us is called Simon. Our father taught us to be true to our king, and to till the ground, and to be kind to our neighbors. He also taught each of us a different trade which he thought might be useful to us, and he bade us not neglect our mother earth, which would be sure amply to repay our labor."

The king was pleased with the honest peasant, and said: "You have done well, good people, in planting your field, and now you have a golden harvest. But I should like each of you to tell me what special trades your father taught you."

"My trade, O king!" said the first Simon, "is not an easy one. If you will give me some workmen and materials I will build you a great white pillar that shall reach far above the clouds."

"Very good," replied the king. "And you, Simon the second, what is your trade?"

"Mine, your Majesty, needs no great cleverness. When my brother has built the pillar I can mount it, and from the top, far above the clouds, I can see what is happening in every country under the sun."

"Good," said the king; "and Simon the third?"

"My work is very simple, sire. You have many ships built by learned men, with all sorts of new and clever improvements. If you wish it I will build you quite a simple boat—one, two, three, and it's done! But my plain little home-made ship is not grand enough for a king. Where other ships take a year, mine makes the voyage in a day, and where they would require ten years mine will do the distance in a week."

"Good," said the king again; "and what has Simon the fourth learnt?"

"My trade, O king, is really of no importance. Should my brother build you a ship, then let me embark in it.

If we should be pursued by an enemy I can seize our boat by the prow and sink it to the bottom of the sea. When the enemy has sailed off, I can draw it up to the top again."

"That is very clever of you," answered the king; "and what does Simon the fifth do?"

"My work, your Majesty, is mere smith's work. Order me to build a smithy and I will make you a cross-bow, but from which neither the eagle in the sky nor the wild beast in the forest is safe. The bolt hits whatever the eye sees."

"That sounds very useful," said the king. "And now, Simon the sixth, tell me your trade."

"Sire, it is so simple I am almost ashamed to mention it. If my brother hits any creature I catch it quicker than any dog can. If it falls into the water I pick it up out of the greatest depths, and if it is in a dark forest I can find it even at midnight."

The king was much pleased with the trades and talk of the six brothers, and said: "Thank you, good people; your father did well to teach you all these things. Now follow me to the town, as I want to see what you can do. I need such people as you about me; but when harvest time comes I will send you home with royal presents."

The brothers bowed and said: "As the king wills." Suddenly the king remembered that he had not questioned the seventh Simon, so he turned to him and said: "Why are you silent? What is your handicraft?"

And the seventh Simon answered: "I have no handicraft, O king; I have learnt nothing. I could not manage it. And if I *do* know how to do anything it is not what might properly be called a real trade—it is rather a sort of performance; but it is one which no one—not the king himself—must watch me doing, and I doubt whether this performance of mine would please your Majesty."

"Come, come," cried the king; "I will have no excuses, what is this trade?"

"First, sire, give me your royal word that you will not kill me when I have told you. Then you shall hear."

"So be it, then; I give you my royal word."

Then the seventh Simon stepped back a little, cleared his throat, and said: "My trade, King Archidej, is of such a kind that the man who follows it in your kingdom generally loses his life and has no hopes of pardon. There is only one thing I can do really well, and that is—to steal, and to hide the smallest scrap of anything I have stolen. Not the deepest vault, even if its lock were enchanted, could prevent my stealing anything out of it that I wished to have."

When the king heard this he fell into a passion. "I will *not* pardon you, you rascal," he cried; "I will shut you up in my deepest dungeon on bread and water till you have forgotten such a trade. Indeed, it would be better to put you to death at once, and I've a good mind to do so."

"Don't kill me, O king! I am really not as bad as you think. Why, had I chosen, I could have robbed the royal treasury, have bribed your judges to let me off, and built a white marble palace with what was left. But though I know how to steal I don't do it. You yourself asked me my trade. If you kill me you will break your royal word."

"Very well," said the king, "I will not kill you. I pardon you. But from this hour you shall be shut up in a dark dungeon. Here, guards! away with him to the prison. But you six Simons follow me and be assured of my royal favor."

So the six Simons followed the king. The seventh Simon

was seized by the guards, who put him in chains and threw him in prison with only bread and water for food. Next day the king gave the first Simon carpenters, masons, smiths, and laborers, with great stores of iron, mortar, and the like, and Simon began to build. And he built his great white pillar far, far up into the clouds, as high as the nearest stars; but the other stars were higher still.

Then the second Simon climbed up the pillar and saw and heard all that was going on through the whole world. When he came down he had all sorts of wonderful things to tell. How one king was marching in battle against another, and which was likely to be the victor. How, in another place, great rejoicings were going on, while in a third people were dying of famine. In fact there was not the smallest event going on over the earth that was hidden from him.

Next the third Simon began. He stretched out his arms, once, twice, thrice, and the wonder-ship was ready. At a sign from the king it was launched, and floated proudly and safely like a bird on the waves. Instead of ropes it had wires for rigging, and musicians played on them with fiddle bows and made lovely music. As the ship swam about, the fourth Simon seized the prow with his strong hand, and in a moment it was gone—sunk to the bottom of the sea. An hour passed, and then the ship floated again, drawn up by Simon's left hand, while in his right he brought a gigantic fish from the depth of the ocean for the royal table.

Whilst this was going on the fifth Simon had built his forge and hammered out his iron, and when the king returned from the harbor the magic cross-bow was made.

His Majesty went out into an open field at once, looked

up into the sky and saw, far, far away, an eagle flying up towards the sun and looking like a little speck.

"Now," said the king, "if you can shoot that bird I will reward you."

Simon only smiled; he lifted his cross-bow, took aim, fired, and the eagle fell. As it was falling the sixth Simon ran with a dish, caught the bird before it fell to earth and brought it to the king.

"Many thanks, my brave lads," said the king; "I see that each of you is indeed a master of his trade. You shall be richly rewarded. But now rest and have your dinner."

The six Simons bowed and went to dinner. But they had hardly begun before a messenger came to say that the king wanted to see them. They obeyed at once and found him surrounded by all his court and men of state.

"Listen, my good fellows," cried the king, as soon as he saw them. "Hear what my wise counsellors have thought of. As you, Simon the second, can see the whole world from the top of the great pillar, I want you to climb up and to see and hear. For I am told that, far away, across many seas, is the great kingdom of the Island of Busan, and that the daughter of the king is the beautiful Princess Helena."

Off ran the second Simon and clambered quickly up the pillar. He gazed around, listened on all sides, and then slid down to report to the king.

"Sire, I have obeyed your orders. Far away I saw the Island of Busan. The king is a mighty monarch, but full of pride, harsh and cruel. He sits on his throne and declares that no prince or king on earth is good enough for his lovely daughter, that he will give her to none, and that if any king asks for her hand he will declare war against him and destroy his kingdom."

"Has the King of Busan a great army?" asked King Archidej; "is his country far off?"

"As far as I could judge," replied Simon, "it would take you nearly ten years in fair weather to sail there. But if the weather were stormy we might say twelve. I saw the army being reviewed. It is not so *very* large—a hundred thousand men at arms and a hundred thousand knights. Besides these, he has a strong bodyguard and a good many cross-bowmen. Altogether you may say another hundred thousand, and there is a picked body of heroes who reserve themselves for great occasions requiring particular courage."

The king sat for some time lost in thought. At last he said to the nobles and courtiers standing around: "I am determined to marry the Princess Helena, but how shall I do it?"

The nobles, courtiers, and counsellors said nothing, but tried to hide behind each other. Then the third Simon said:

"Pardon me, your Majesty, if I offer my advice. You wish to go to the Island of Busan? What can be easier? In my ship you will get there in a week instead of in ten years. But ask your council to advise you what to do when you arrive—in one word, whether you will win the princess peacefully or by war?"

But the wise men were as silent as ever.

The king frowned, and was about to say something sharp, when the Court Fool pushed his way to the front and said: "Dear me, what are all you clever people so puzzled about? The matter is quite clear. As it seems it will not take long to reach the island why not send the seventh Simon? He will steal the fair maiden fast enough, and then the king, her father, may consider how he is going to bring his army over here—it will take him ten years to do it!—no less! What do you think of my plan?"

"What do I think? Why, that your idea is capital, and you shall be rewarded for it. Come, guards, hurry as fast as you can and bring the seventh Simon before me."

Not many minutes later, Simon the seventh stood before the king, who explained to him what he wished done, and also that to steal for the benefit of his king and country was by no means a wrong thing, though it was very wrong to steal for his own advantage.

The youngest Simon, who looked very pale and hungry, only nodded his head.

"Come," said the king, "tell me truly. Do you think you could steal the Princess Helena?"

"Why should I not steal her, sire? The thing is easy enough. Let my brother's ship be laden with rich stuffs, brocades, Persian carpets, pearls, and jewels. Send me in the ship. Give me my four middle brothers as companions, and keep the two others as hostages."

When the king heard these words his heart became filled with longing, and he ordered all to be done as Simon wished. Everyone ran about to do his bidding; and in next to no time the wonder-ship was laden and ready to start.

The five Simons took leave of the king, went on board, and had no sooner set sail than they were almost out of sight. The ship cut through the waters like a falcon through the air, and just a week after starting sighted the Island of Busan. The coast appeared to be strongly guarded, and from afar the watchman on a high tower called out: "Halt and anchor! Who are you? Where do you come from, and what do you want?"

The seventh Simon answered from the ship: "We are

peaceful people. We come from the country of the great
and good King Archidej, and we bring foreign wares—
rich brocades, carpets, and costly jewels, which we wish
to show to your king and the princess. We desire to trade
—to sell, to buy, and to exchange."

The brothers launched a small boat, took some of their
valuable goods with them, rowed to shore and went up to
the palace. The princess sat in a rose-red room, and when
she saw the brothers coming near she called her nurse
and other women, and told them to inquire who and
what these people were, and what they wanted.

The seventh Simon answered the nurse: "We come

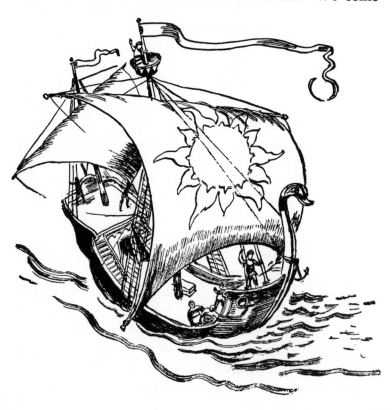

from the country of the wise and good King Archidej,"
said he, "and we have brought all sorts of goods for sale.
We trust the king of this country may condescend to
welcome us, and to let his servants take charge of our
wares. If he considers them worthy to adorn his followers
we shall be content."

This speech was repeated to the princess, who ordered
the brothers to be brought to the red room at once. They
bowed respectfully to her and displayed some splendid
velvets and brocades, and opened cases of pearls and
precious stones. Such beautiful things had never been
seen in the island, and the nurse and waiting women
stood bewildered by all the magnificence. They whispered together that they had never beheld anything like
it. The princess too saw and wondered, and her eyes
could not weary of looking at the lovely things, or her
fingers of stroking the rich soft stuffs, and of holding up
the sparkling jewels to the light.

"Fairest of princesses," said Simon, "be pleased to
order your waiting-maids to accept the silks and velvets,
and let your women trim their head-dresses with the
jewels; these are no special treasures. But permit me to
say that they are as nothing to the many colored tapes-
tries, the gorgeous stones and ropes of pearls in our ship.
We did not like to bring more with us, not knowing what
your royal taste might be; but if it seems good to you to
honor our ship with a visit, you might condescend to
choose such things as were pleasing in your eyes."

This polite speech pleased the princess very much.
She went to the king and said: "Dear father, some merchants have arrived with the most splendid wares. Pray
allow me to go to their ship and choose out what I like."

The king thought and thought, frowned hard and

rubbed his ear. At last he gave consent, and ordered out his royal yacht, with 100 cross-bows, 100 knights, and 1,000 soldiers, to escort the Princess Helena.

Off sailed the yacht with the princess and her escort. The brothers Simon came on board to conduct the princess to their ship, and, led by the brothers and followed by her nurse and other women, she crossed the crystal plank from one vessel to another.

The seventh Simon spread out his goods, and had so many curious and interesting tales to tell about them, that the princess forgot everything else in looking and listening, so that she did not know that the fourth Simon had seized the prow of the ship, and that all of a sudden it had vanished from sight, and was racing along in the depths of the sea.

The crew of the royal yacht shouted aloud, the knights stood still with terror, the soldiers were struck dumb and hung their heads. There was nothing to be done but to sail back and tell the king of his loss.

How he wept and stormed! "Oh, light of my eyes," he sobbed; "I am indeed punished for my pride. I thought no one good enough to be your husband, and now you are lost in the depths of the sea, and have left me alone! As for all of you who saw this thing—away with you! Let them be put in irons and lock them up in prison, whilst I think how I can best put them to death!"

Whilst the King of Busan was raging and lamenting in this fashion, Simon's ship was swimming like any fish under the sea, and when the island was well out of sight he brought it up to the surface again. At that moment the princess recollected herself. "Nurse," said she, "we have been gazing at these wonders only too long. I hope my father won't be vexed at our delay."

She tore herself away and stepped on deck. Neither
the yacht nor the island was in sight! Helena wrung her
hands and beat her breast. Then she changed herself into
a white swan and flew off. But the fifth Simon seized his
bow and shot the swan, and the sixth Simon did not let
it fall into the water but caught it in the ship, and the
swan turned into a silver fish, but Simon lost no time and
caught the fish, when, quick as thought, the fish turned
into a black mouse and ran about the ship. It darted towards a hole, but before it could reach it Simon sprang
upon it more swiftly than any cat, and then the little
mouse turned once more into the beautiful Princess
Helena.

Early one morning King Archidej sat thoughtfully at
his window gazing out to sea. His heart was sad and he
would neither eat nor drink. His thoughts were full of
the Princess Helena, who was as lovely as a dream. Is
that a white gull he sees flying towards the shore, or is it
a sail? No, it is no gull, it is the wonder-ship flying along
with billowing sails. Its flags wave, the fiddlers play on
the wire rigging, the anchor is thrown out and the crystal
plank laid from the ship to the pier. The lovely Helena
steps across the plank. She shines like the sun, and the
stars of heaven seem to sparkle in her eyes.

Up sprang King Archidej in haste: "Hurry, hurry," he
cried. "Let us hasten to meet her! Let the bugles sound
and the joy bells be rung!"

And the whole Court swarmed with courtiers and servants. Golden carpets were laid down and the great gates
thrown open to welcome the princess.

King Archidej went out himself, took her by the hand
and led her into the royal apartments.

"Madam," said he, "the fame of your beauty had

reached me, but I had not dared to expect such loveliness. Still I will not keep you here against your will. If you wish it, the wonder-ship shall take you back to your father and your own country; but if you will consent to stay here, then reign over me and my country as our queen."

What more is there to tell? It is not hard to guess that the princess listened to the king's wooing, and their betrothal took place with great pomp and rejoicings.

The brothers Simon were sent again to the Island of Busan with a letter to the king from his daughter to invite him to their wedding. And the wonder-ship arrived at the Island of Busan just as all the knights and soldiers who had escorted the princess were being led out to execution.

Then the seventh Simon cried out from the ship: "Stop! stop! I bring a letter from the Princess Helena!"

The King of Busan read the letter over and over again, and ordered the knights and soldiers to be set free. He entertained King Archidej's ambassadors hospitably, and sent his blessing to his daughter, but he could not be brought to attend the wedding.

When the wonder-ship got home King Archidej and Princess Helena were enchanted with the news it brought.

The king sent for the seven Simons. "A thousand thanks to you, my brave fellows," he cried. "Take what gold, silver, and precious stones you will out of my treasury. Tell me if there is anything else you wish for and I will give it you, my good friends. Do you wish to be made nobles, or to govern towns? Only speak."

Then the eldest Simon bowed and said: "We are plain folk, your Majesty, and understand simple things best. What figures should we cut as nobles or governors? Nor do we desire gold. We have our fields which give us food, and as much money as we need. If you wish to reward us then grant that our land may be free of taxes, and of your goodness pardon the seventh Simon. He is not the first who has been a thief by trade and he will certainly not be the last."

"So be it," said the king; "your land shall be free of all taxes, and Simon the seventh is pardoned."

Then the king gave each brother a goblet of wine and invited them to the wedding feast. And *what* a feast that was!

5

THREE FRIDAYS

◇◇

"THE THIRD FRIDAY FOUND HIM ONCE MORE
CLIMBING THE PULPIT STEPS WITH NOT A
WORD WORTH SAYING IN THAT SOLEMN
MOSQUE."

◇◇

There was just one day of each week that worried Nasr-ed-Din Hodja. On six days he was as free as a butterfly. He could talk with his friends in the market place or ride his donkey to a nearby village. He could work in the vineyards or go hunting in the hills. He could lounge in the coffee house or sit in the sun in his own courtyard. There was nothing to hurry him to be at a certain place at a certain time to do a certain thing.

But Friday was different. It was much different. That was the day when all good Mohammedans went to their mosques. Because Nasr-ed-Din Hodja, years before, had attended the school for priests, he was expected each Friday to mount the pulpit of the mosque at a certain time and preach a sermon. That was all very well when he had something to say, but there were many Fridays

[55]

when his mind was as empty as that of his own little gray
donkey. It was one thing to swap stories with the men in
the coffee house and quite another to stand alone in the
high pulpit and talk to a mosque full of people. The men,
each squatting on his own prayer rug on the floor, looked
up at him with such solemn faces. Then there was the
fluttering in the balcony behind the lattices, which told
him that the women were waiting too. Of course, the
chanting, which came before the sermon, was not hard
because all the men joined in that, bowing till they
touched their foreheads to the floor in the Nemaz. But
the sermon—that was hard.

One Friday he walked more slowly than ever through
the cobblestoned streets of Ak Shehir. He saw the veiled
women slipping silently past him on their way to the
latticed balcony of the mosque. He saw the men in their
best clothes hurrying to the mosque to hear his sermon.
But what sermon? He stopped at the mosque door to
leave his shoes. He pattered with the other men across
the soft thick rugs. But they could squat on the rugs,
while he had to climb into the high pulpit.

Perhaps the beauty of the mosque would give him an
idea. He looked up at the blues and reds and whites of
the intricate tracery on the ceiling, but not a thought
came. He looked at the rich yellows and reds of the mosaics on the walls, but there was no help there. He looked
at the men's faces staring up at him. He heard the titter-
ing in the latticed balcony where the veiled women sat.
He must say something.

"Oh, people of Ak Shehir!" He leaned on the pulpit
and eyed them squarely. "Do you know what I am about
to say to you?"

"No!" boomed from the rugs where the men squatted.

"No!" floated down in soft whispers from the latticed balcony, whispers not meant for any ears beyond the balcony.

"You do not know?" said Nasr-ed-Din Hodja, shaking his head and looking from one face to another. "You are sure you do not know? Then what use would it be to talk to people who know nothing at all about this important subject. My words would be wasted on such ignorant people."

With that, the Hodja turned and climbed slowly down the pulpit steps. His eyes lowered, he walked with injured dignity through the crowds of men. He slipped on his shoes at the mosque door, and was out in the sunshine —free until next Friday.

That day came all too soon. The Hodja mingled with the crowds going to the mosque. His coarse, home-knit stockings pattered across the deep colorful rugs. He climbed the steps to the high pulpit. He looked down at the sea of solemn faces. He heard the rustling behind the lattices of the balcony. He had hoped that this week he could think of a sermon, but the carvings of the doorway did not help him, nor the embroidered hangings of the pulpit, nor the pigeons fluttering and cooing at the window. Still, he must say something.

"Oh, people of Ak Shehir!" intoned the Hodja, gesturing with both hands. "Do you know what I am about to say to you?"

"Yes," boomed the men who remembered what had happened when they said "No" last week.

"Yes," echoed in soft whispers from the balcony.

"You know what I am going to say?" said the Hodja, shrugging first one shoulder and then the other. "You are sure you know what I am going to say? Then I need

not say it. It would be a useless waste of my golden words if I told you something that you already knew."

The Hodja turned and again climbed down the pulpit steps. He picked his way with unhurried dignity among the men. He scuffed into his shoes and escaped into the sunshine. Another free week was ahead of him.

But the best of weeks end. The third Friday found him

once more climbing the pulpit steps, with not a word worth saying in that solemn mosque. The ancient Arabic writing on the bright ceiling had no help for him. The flickering candles in the large round chandelier winked at him but said nothing. Even the big Koran in front of him might have had blank pages instead of its fine Arabic words and its illuminated borders. Men's faces looked up at him expectantly. Bright eyes peered through the lattices of the women's balcony. The time had come again when he must speak.

"Oh, people of Ak Shehir!" declaimed the Hodja as he groped helplessly for an idea. "Do you know what I am about to say to you?"

"No," came from those who were thinking of the last Friday.

"Yes," came from those who were thinking of the Friday before that.

"Some of you know and some of you do not know!" The Hodja rubbed his hands together and beamed down at the men. "How very fine! Now let those who know tell those who do not know!"

The Hodja was humming to himself as he came down from the pulpit, two steps at a time. He nodded and smiled as he threaded his way through the men. Some thought he bowed and smiled toward the latticed balcony, but others said the good Hodja would not have made so bold. He picked his own worn shoes from the rows and rows by the mosque door. The sunshine was warm and friendly. The birds were singing and there was the fragrance of hawthorn blossoms in the air.

The Hodja had not a worry in the world—not till another Friday should come around.

6

THE TURQUOISE PRINCESS

"I WOULD HAVE YOU MARRY A PRINCESS WHO
IS BOTH BEAUTIFUL AND HARD-WORKING, FOR
A QUEEN WHO THINKS ONLY OF PLEASURE AND
FINE CLOTHES WILL NEVER HELP YOU RULE
WISELY."

Once upon a time there was an old and widowed queen who had an only son, and feeling that her age prevented her from giving as much care as she had formerly done to the affairs of her state, she called the young Prince to her.

"My son," she said, "before death calls me to another world I would like to see you happily married, and to give the lands over to you and your wife, for the time has come when you must put pleasure to one side and shoulder the responsibility of your high estate. I would have you marry a princess who is both beautiful and hard-working, for a queen who thinks only of pleasure

and fine clothes will never help you to rule wisely, therefore, choose a maiden who can be queenly and yet simple.

"Now I know of three sisters, the daughters of a king.
They live at a great distance from here. Rumor has it that
all three are fair and diligent. The eldest is called Gold,
the second Conch Shell, and the youngest and most beautiful, Turquoise. In choosing one of these maidens be
guided by her character rather than by her fairness of
face."

And saying this she took the Prince to a closet, and
taking out a casket, opened it and gave him three rings.
One was of plain gold, the other made of conch shell,
and the third was made of turquoise.

"Whatever you do," said the Queen, "keep these rings
carefully. Hide them and let no one see them except the
three Princesses. You cannot help but fall in love with one
of them, and to that chosen maid you must give the ring
which is the symbol of her name."

The Queen then gave the Prince rich clothing, a milk-
white horse to ride, and a servant to walk beside him,
who would attend to his requirements on the road.

The Prince and the servant set forth and journeyed
many days and nights. This servant had always been a
favorite with the Prince, and as they were wandering on
their way they talked together to pass the time. Though
the Prince had been warned by his mother to keep the
purpose of his journey secret, he began to talk to the
servant very freely, telling him about the three Princesses, that they were rich and beautiful and that he was
going to woo one of them.

Now the servant, who pretended to be so faithful and
servile, was in reality a most cunning and evil fellow who
had made up his mind before the Prince set off to murder

his master and decamp with the money bags, and for this dark purpose had concealed a sharp sword inside his tunic. He had also induced the Prince to part with his own dagger which he wore fastened to his belt, saying that he would carry it for the Prince until he had need of it, as he had a soft woolen cloth in which he would wrap it to keep the steel from rusting, which it would do when the mountain mists touched it. "For," said he, "if a spot of rust was to show on my master's dagger they would say at the Court that I was a careless servant, and being proud of my master's appearance I would have him shine from top to toe."

The Prince smiled and thought how fortunate a man he was to have a servant who thought for him even to so small a detail as a speck of rust.

"My good fellow," he said, "if all goes well with us you shall be amply rewarded when we return," and he went on chatting with his servant, telling him that he was not known to the father of the Princesses and wished to make a good impression on him from the start, so that, if it chanced that he asked for one of the sisters in marriage, the King would not refuse him her hand.

The servant thought over what the Prince had told him and said to himself: "He promises to reward me well *if* all goes well with him, but if not, I stand a chance of getting nothing. If, indeed! There shall be no *ifs* about it, for I shall help myself to my own reward," and thinking thus, he conceived a plot.

The kingdom to which the two were traveling was surrounded on all sides by lofty mountain ranges, so, to get there, the Prince and the servant were forced to cross over a high and lonely pass. The servant, being a hillsman, knew that the passes were guarded by demons who were invisible but had the power to suck the breath of a man, causing him to suffer from weakness and giddiness, and so sapping his strength that he became as helpless, often, as a babe. In his own pocket he carried an herb that the demons particularly disliked owing to its pungent odor. The Prince being a man of the plains, the servant thought he would readily succumb to the influence of the demons, and more so as he knew nothing of the powers of the herb, and feeling a shortness of breath would become the demons' prey, and without knowing what it was that caused his discomfort, gasp for air, give up his breath to them, and in return have his lungs filled with the poisons that they exhaled from their own. In this he was right, for though the Prince was by no means a weakling, when they got to the highest point of the pass and could see the turrets of the palace in the valley below shining like golden spears in the sun, and knew that by night they would be at their journey's end, the Prince began to gasp like a fish that gets washed up out of a lake, and complained to his servant, saying, "Let us halt here awhile until I feel better, for I have been overtaken by sickness."

The servant, who had been chewing the herb, had breathed nothing in but the pure mountain air, so the demons would not go near him, and he felt his strength doubled to fit him for the evil task he had set himself.

"Do not remain upon your horse, sir," said the servant. "I will help you to dismount."

The Prince dismounted, saying, "My good man, do not distress yourself at my sickness. With a short rest I will feel better, and we can then continue the journey."

"I'm not troubling about you," said the servant rudely, springing at the Prince and knocking him down. "And I would have you know that unless you lie quiet your own dagger will not hang at your side again, but be thrust through your heart to gather rust there up to the hilt."

The unfortunate Prince saw his servant's treachery, but knew he was in the man's power. Weak as he was, he would have fought to defend himself had he had his dagger, but he well knew that only his wits could now save him, for his servant had his dagger as well as the sword which he brandished over his unfortunate victim, who had only his naked hands to defend himself with.

"Before I kill you," said the servant, "make haste and get out of those satin robes. I am going to put them on myself, they will suit me well," and he chuckled, and mimicking his master said, "I must present myself at the Court looking my best, so the King will not refuse me the hand of his daughter."

The Prince took his rich clothes off and gave them to the servant, who put them on and threw his coarse ones to the Prince, saying, "You may as well have an extra stitch to cover you, for you'll be cold enough when you're dead."

"Since I have nothing to turn on you but my tongue,"

said the Prince, who had been busy thinking out a plan
to save himself from having his life cut short by his servant's sword, "I can tell you that you may as well kill me
quickly and go back home, for no king would believe
you to be anything but the traitorous scoundrel you are.
A real prince does not travel without a servant."

"That's so," said the servant, "and since I have been
induced to alter my plans once to win a royal damsel to
wife, I may as well change my plans a second time. Thank
you for reminding me. A good appearance goes a long
way, and I daresay you would rather accompany me as
my servant than to be left behind to sleep in the snow.
But my old rags are unsuited to your fair skin. However,
I have something to remedy that in my pocket," and he
took out a ball of brown wax and made the Prince smear
it over his hands and face. "Ah! that looks better, and
you'll do very well," said he, when the Prince was thickly
smeared with the dirty wax. "Now we can go on"; and
he jumped on his master's horse.

The Prince said nothing more, but he thought to himself, "My foolish tongue has got me into difficulties, but
luckily it has got me out easier than I thought. I will keep
a curb on it." And he dragged after the servant without
uttering a word.

That night the two travelers arrived at the city walls.
It was late. The watchman, hearing a knock, called,
"Who goes there?"

"A prince to woo a princess," replied the servant
boldly, and the watchman, looking through the window
of the watchtower, and seeing a stranger in satin robes
riding on a richly caparisoned horse with a servant in
attendance, hurried down, and bowing profusely, opened
the gates to let the visitors pass, and bade them welcome.

The wicked servant inquired where the best inn was to be found, and, being told, they made their way towards it.

"Stay where you are," said he to the Prince, "while I go and find the landlord: and mind you keep your mouth shut. If you don't it will be shut for you."

"In what a position I find myself," thought the Prince. "No doubt the impudent fellow imagines that his outward splendor and the power he has usurped from me allows him to be insolent, his vulgar mind conceiving such conduct to be a princely attribute, though from me, who am a prince, he received nothing but gentleness and courtesy."

"Here is the man," said the servant, returning shortly with the landlord. "Clap the chains round his ankles and lead him to the cowshed to sleep for the night. He looks meek enough standing there, but his meekness is only feigned. He's as unruly a scamp as you'd get anywhere. And if in the morning you want a goat-herd, you are welcome to his services for nothing. It will do him good to be kept busy while I go about my business."

So it was arranged that the poor Prince was to be chained up for the night, and in the morning was to be sent out to mind the innkeeper's goats.

"Nothing I can say will make me believed," thought the Prince. "So the best thing I can do is to remain dumb and await my opportunity to get together enough food to cover my needs for a return journey, and then escape. Whatever task I am given I will do it to the best of my ability. The innkeeper may, seeing my worth, pay me a wage."

Next morning early the innkeeper came along and unchained the Prince. "You're a good-looking youth," he said. "It's a pity you've crossed your master, for there's little doubt he's a person of great importance. I'm not a hard man, but I've got to carry out my orders, or trouble will fall on my head. Your master says you're to have nothing to eat until noon, when he himself will leave you something in the corner of the field." He led the Prince some distance to a field, and showing him the goats, said, "Here are your charges. If you allow one to stray, or your herd to get mixed in with another herd, at night, when you bring them in, you will get a beating."

The Prince was glad to be out of the stuffy and evil-smelling cowshed. He had hardly slept a wink all night, for the restlessness of the cattle had kept him awake, and he was not long lying in the grass watching the flock when his head began to nod, and he fell asleep.

When he awoke the sun was high in the heavens. He looked about him. There was not a single goat to be seen. The Prince scrambled to his feet. "This will never do," he thought. "However came it that I gave in to my drowsiness? The first day I am sent out to mind the goats I lose not one but the whole flock."

While the Prince was acting as goat-herd the traitorous servant was playing Prince in great style. He presented himself at the Palace and was very well received there. He put on such grand airs, and accepted all that was done for him with such an indifference, that the King said to the Queen, "His kingdom must be at least double the size of ours."

"It must be," said the Queen, "but his mother has brought him up badly, for even if he thought our kingdom mean in comparison with his own, he need not show it while he is our guest."

"It would be unwise to cross him," said the King. "For

if his kingdom is twice the size of our kingdom, he will have twice the number of troops."

The servant was not long making his business known to the King and Queen. "I have come," he said, "to ask for the hand of one of your daughters. I hear that you have three and all are beautiful. The most beautiful of your three beautiful daughters I would take to wife. Mine is a rich and prosperous kingdom and the envy of princes far and wide."

"I had," said the King, "three beautiful daughters. To the Queen and myself one was not more beautiful than the other. Of these three daughters two are married. I have but one left, the Princess Turquoise. She is said to be the fairest and the most difficult to please. If you can find favor in her eyes we will give our consent. Many are the princes who have wooed her, but none has won her. Not a week passes but that a prince comes here to ask for her hand."

The servant thought of the bags of money he could spill at the Princess Turquoise's feet, and made sure when she saw the heap of gold she would consent to marry him.

When the Princess Turquoise heard that yet another suitor was waiting to see her she said disdainfully, "He may wait. I will not see him."

"I insist," said her father, "that you behave properly. This prince is rich and powerful, and if you treat him disdainfully he may become ill-humored and wage war against us. From his appearance and the ease with which I am told he spends his money, I do not doubt but what he could provide handsomely for you."

"He is neither good-mannered nor good-looking," said the Princess, who had hidden behind a screen when her suitor entered and had seen and heard all that had passed. "I would rather give my hand to a scullion than give it to him. The riches of his kingdom will not buy my love."

"He certainly has bad manners," said the Queen. "But it would be unwise to annoy him by letting him see you notice his faults. He looks as if he could easily be roused to anger. Therefore, show yourself prepared to meet his wishes, but tell him you must be allowed time to think over his suit, and ask him to return in a month for your answer."

"In a month or a year," said the Princess, "I should be of the same mind, so what use to tell him that?"

"Wayward girl," said the King, "your disdain may cost us our kingdom."

So determined was the Princess not to speak to her suitor that the next morning early she dressed herself as a village maid, and taking a flock of her father's goats, she went on to the hillside knowing that no one would ever suspect, finding her there. The poor Prince was in the adjoining field and was keeping a close watch on his goats, for he had had a severe trouncing the night before for allowing them to stray, and had no wish to have another, but when the Princess's goats began to graze the Prince's goats ran off to join them. The Prince followed after the goats as fast as he could, and seeing a girl standing among them, went up to her with the purpose of asking her to help him separate her goats from his. From her dress he supposed her to be a goat girl, but when she turned round and he saw her beautiful face, he quickly dropped his head and gazed on the ground, feeling ashamed that she should look at him in his dirty and ragged clothes.

"Are these your goats?" asked the Princess, who had

experienced a strange thrill when she looked into the Prince's eyes.

"Yes," said the Prince, "they are my goats." And he said nothing more, but stood there while the color mounted to his cheeks and glowed dully through the dirty wax that smeared them.

"What ails you, boy?" said the Princess. "And why do you stand dumbly looking at the ground?"

"Fair maid," replied the Prince, "do not ask me, for I cannot answer you, but pray call your goats to you."

The Princess's heart was filled with compassion, for she noticed that the young goat-herd looked weak and sad. "Come," said she kindly, "let us share our food together and then separate our flocks when we have eaten."

Now the Prince had only a handful of corn and a dog's leg, which the wicked servant had thrown to him. The dog's leg he had buried, and the corn he had eaten, so he had nothing to offer. He shook his head and walked quickly away, calling to his goats to follow him. At first the Princess thought the goat-herd did not wish to give her any of his food, and then, remembering how sorrowful he looked, she guessed that he had none to give her and blamed herself for asking him.

That night the Princess could not sleep for thinking of the goat-herd. In vain she told herself that he was dirty and ragged, but notwithstanding he filled her thoughts and her dreams, and as soon as it was daylight she donned her peasant's robe and hastened to the field to await him, only to meet with disappointment, for the wicked servant had heard that the Prince had been seen wandering up the hill, and ordered him to take his goats to a more distant field, and threatened to kill him if he was seen leaving it.

The Prince tethered his goats, but the poor fellow could not tether his thoughts, for he had fallen in love with the Princess Turquoise the moment he had set eyes on her, and his thoughts had followed her every moment since.

"If I told her that I was a prince she would not believe me," he thought, "and if she did believe me, being only a peasant girl herself, she would be afraid."

The Princess, on her hill slope, was thinking much the same thing. "If he knew I was a princess he would be afraid to speak to me, and if my parents knew, I would be held a captive and he would be flogged."

The days went on, and the Princess Turquoise could think of nothing at all but the strange goat-herd, and the more she thought of him, the more deeply did she fall in love with him, and the more sure was she that he was keeping away purposely because, though he thought she was only a peasant maid, he could see she was not as poor and humble as he was.

"If only I could see him once again," said the Princess to herself, "I would be so humble that he would no longer mind speaking to me," and she cried out to the goats, "Goats, goats, lead me to my goat-herd." She said this more to relieve her heart of its cruel ache than anything else, so when the goats pricked up their ears and began forming themselves into line, and walked solemnly two by two, as if they understood what was required of them, no one could have been more surprised than the Princess herself. But she followed them, her heart going pit-a-pat all the while. On and on went the little procession, over the green hills and down the valleys, never loitering to munch by the way until they had led the Princess to the Prince's side.

The little Princess tried to hide her feelings, and said, "I have come here to ask you to consent to share our meal together," and opening a napkin in which was some food, set it in front of the Prince.

The tears welled up in the Prince's eyes. "Sweet maid," he said, "how can I tell you? Yet I must. All I have is a dog's leg and a handful of corn thrown to me daily. The dog's leg I bury, the corn I must eat, for hunger drives me to it."

The Prince looked dirtier and more unkempt than ever. His tousled hair, which he wore in braids round his head, was matted together, and pieces of straw and dead leaves showed in it from having slept in the cowshed, where he was forced to gather straw and leaves nightly to make himself a pillow to rest his head.

The Princess drew the Prince down beside her. "I have more than enough for myself here," she said. "How can I eat, knowing you have nothing?"

"And how," replied the Prince, "can I eat with you, for when I think how dirty I look I am overcome with shame. Your gentle heart has been kindled by pity, but I am not fit company for one so fair."

"I care not for that," said the Princess, her love making her bold. " 'Twas not pity that brought me here but—" She stopped, and hid her face in her hands, as if she could say no more, and taking a comb from her dark tresses, she asked the Prince to let her comb and braid his hair neatly, and without giving him time to say "yea" or "nay," she lifted her hands and uncoiled one of his thick braids. As it fell something fell with it. The three rings which the Prince for safety had tied together and hidden in his hair. The Princess picked them up.

"What is this," she exclaimed, "that you have here?

Three rings—gold, conch shell, and turquoise? The first is the name of my elder sister, Gold, the second is the name of my second sister, Conch Shell, and this, the third, is my own name, Turquoise. How came you to have these rings?"

The Prince then realized that the beautiful lady who had captured his heart was none other than the Princess Turquoise. He knelt at her feet and offered her the turquoise ring, saying: "Princess, I was not always the dirty beggar you now see kneeling before you. In the cold my face is black, but were I to stand in the warmth my skin would become fair. If only I could prove my words to you, but, alas, I cannot."

"You shall do so," said the Princess. "To-night, when the world is asleep, come to the Palace. On the right you will see a small door. I will leave it unlatched. Creep in quietly and mount the winding stair. It will bring you to my room. I will have a great fire blazing on the hearth there, and you shall sit before it and tell me the meaning of your mysterious words."

Fortune favored the Prince. The innkeeper, by happy chance, was kept busy attending on late arrivals and forgot to pass by the cattle shed the last thing to chain the Prince up, as was his custom, the fact being that the good host was overwhelmed at the number of lordly visitors who had arrived at the hostelry, and was at his wit's end to know where to accommodate them all. The Princess Turquoise's beauty had been noised so far abroad that princes from the North, South, East and West of the world were arriving at her father's kingdom, all hoping to carry off so prized a gem as this princess, who was said to be so beautiful and so disdainful.

Dark glances flashed from one to the other of the new-

comers, and each wondered if his neighbor would find
favor in her eyes, while yet picturing himself the jealous
center, on which all eyes would be set when the lovely
Princess consented to place her white hand in his and
ride away from her father's realm. There were fat princes,
and thin princes, short princes and tall ones slumbering
under the innkeeper's hospitable roof that night, dream-
ing of a princess—a princess who, while they dreamed of
her, was piling logs on the fire and listening for the footsteps of her goat-herd.

As soon as it was dark the Prince crept out of the cowshed and, making sure that there was nobody about, stole
to the Palace. He found the little door open a crack, and
pushing it wider mounted the stair and reached the room.
A great fire was blazing on the hearth, and beside it stood
the Princess, so radiantly lovely that the Prince could
scarcely believe his eyes. She had changed her coarse
peasant's dress for one of rich brocade, and round her
head was an aureole of turquoise and pearl.

"Princess," exclaimed the Prince, dropping on his
bended knees, and he kissed her naked feet. "You have
made me slave to your gentleness, and now you make me
slave to your beauty."

"Tell me what manner of goat-herd is he," whispered
the Princess, kneeling beside him, "whose voice so belies
his calling?"

And while the Prince told his story the fierce heat
melted the black disfiguring grease and revealed to the
Princess the pale handsome face of her lover. Until dawn
the Prince and Princess spoke together, and many promises and words of endearment were exchanged between
them. Then, knowing it would be unwise to stay longer,
the Prince took leave of the Princess.

Returning to the dirty hovel he again smeared his face over with black grease and resolved to wait patiently until he and the Princess Turquoise could find an opportunity to flee, for they had plighted their troth, and the Princess had vowed she would marry him and no other.

News of the arrivals of princes from the four quarters of the world reached the ears of the King early, and being much disturbed he made his way to his daughter's apartment and roused her from her sleep.

"Your unseemly conduct," said the King, "brings me here at this early hour to speak with you. I demand to know where you hide yourself during the day."

"My father," said the Princess, "I have been on the hillside with your goats, preferring the life of a simple maid to that of a princess forced to speak fair words to an unwanted suitor."

The King, on hearing this, became exceedingly wrathful with the Princess. "You have reached the age," said he, "when you must choose a husband. Assembled at this hour in my kingdom are princes from the world over. From among them you must make a choice before the sun sets this night. I shall post guards at your door. The waiting women shall dress you in your best, and you shall be carried to the market place, there to receive your suitors and announce your choice."

True to his threat the King sent forth the Royal criers to proclaim his will that his daughter, the Princess Turquoise, would choose from among the princes assembled one for husband. At the appointed hour crowds collected, and the Princess was drawn in a golden chaise and made to seat herself on the pile of cushions placed on a throne in the center of the market place. Decked in jewels from head to foot, the lovely young Princess was acclaimed by the multitudes, who jostled and craned their necks in an endeavor to get a better look at her.

"Whom will she choose?" was the question on all lips, as one by one the princely suitors made their obeisance and filed past.

The Princess Turquoise sat upon her throne like a graven image. The King, her father, watched her closely, hoping to see a flicker of interest lighten her marble countenance. He soon perceived that the Princess did not cast a glance on any of her suitors, but stared fixedly into space above their heads. It became apparent to even the greatest dullard among the crowd that the Princess had no intention whatever of selecting a husband.

The Princess had not behaved as the King had expected, and he was obliged to admit to himself that he was at a loss to know what to do with her, but naturally he did not wish to admit this, so he said in an undertone to the Princess, "Which of these handsome young men will you have for your husband?"

"How can I tell you?" replied the Princess. "I have not seen one of them."

The King knew that what the Princess said was very true, but since he had announced that his daughter was going to choose a husband, he felt he must satisfy the expectant throng.

"My good people," said the King, "the Princess Turquoise is overwhelmed by the number of suitors who have paid homage to her this day. It will be perceived that her mind is divided equally among them. At no time has it been known that so many illustrious and worthy princes have at once been gathered together in a kingdom to woo a lady. Were I to be asked the one I would like as my son-in-law, seeing that all are equally hand-

some and to be desired, I should find myself unable to
choose. Therefore, I would have it known that to-morrow
at the same hour I will have the Great Divining Elephant
brought in your midst, and he shall pick out the rightful
husband for my daughter."

Thereupon the crowds were dispersed, and the Princess was borne back weeping to the Palace. The innkeeper, who had been one of the crowd, was full of talk
—he talked over the affair with everyone who would have
a word with him. He even made it his business to go to
the cowshed to discuss the matter with the goat-herd.

"You should have been there," said he, "and seen the
King's daughter; she was as white as a piece of marble,
and every bit as cold. I'll warrant she's having a scolding
this minute. The King was hard put by to know what to
say, but His Majesty was exceedingly discreet."

"Give me leave to go to the market place to-morrow,"
said the young Prince. "You shall never rue it."

"Hump," said the innkeeper, "I don't know so much
about that. What if your master discovers your absence?"

The Prince pleaded very earnestly with the innkeeper,
who at length consented, provided he promised faithfully to keep well at the back of the crowd.

"You may rest assured," said the Prince, "that I will
give you my word and keep to it. My master gave me a
bad character, but you have known me long enough to
judge me for yourself. True, there have been occasions
when I have allowed my goats to stray, but never will-
fully. I have taken my punishments with a good grace,
and at no time have I borne you malice. I get no wage for
my services, and I have asked for none. Grant me but
one request, for though I am unkempt and dirty I am as
other men who are more favored. Beauty lures me as it

does them, and I would fain look upon the face of the Princess Turquoise, who is said to be the fairest and most disdainful of all women."

The innkeeper shuffled off rubbing his hands. "A rat must creep sometimes out of his hole," he thought, "and that ragged youth deserves better treatment than he gets; his master will never know I let him go, he will be too anxious to push himself in the front of the ranks to occupy himself with his miserable servant."

Neither the Prince in his cow byre nor the Princess in her palace slept—the Princess for thinking she would never see her lover more, and the Prince for thinking it would be the last time he would be permitted to look on her fair face.

The dreaded day dawned. The two lovers bade farewell to hope. Beautiful, in spite of the tears that stained her peach-like cheeks, the Princess Turquoise was conducted once more to the market place, where her princely and unwanted suitors anxiously awaited her coming. Full of eagerness and curiosity, the people, to whom this spectacle was a feast of amusement, waved and cheered. Yesterday the Princess had been dressed in gold and silver; to-day she wore robes of turquoise blue. Ropes of turquoise were wound round her slender throat. The same heaven-sent stone was plaited through her dark hair. Her hands alone were bare of ornament, save for one ring, the band of blue turquoise that her lover had given her the day when he and she had sat together in the green fields, a simple man and maid discovering the secrets of one another's hearts.

There was a loud blare of trumpets as the Great Divining Elephant drew near. To the Princess the frightful

noise sounded like the notes of horns blown over the
tombs of dead men, and she was seen to shiver, for in
very truth it was to her as if they were sounding the
mournful knell of her own unhappy self.

Never was the Great Divining Elephant called but on
great occasions. That the King should ask him to choose
a husband for his daughter proved beyond dispute that
he and his councilors had been unable to solve the prob-
lem themselves. They were agreed that the Princess must
marry sooner or later, and they were agreed that the
sooner she was married the better for the peace of the
entire kingdom. For, as the Chief Councilor had said,
and not without reason, "Each princeling the Princess
flouts leaves here with his pride injured and doubtless
inclined to seek revenge."

"The Elephant will choose! The Elephant will choose!"
shouted the people.

The King mounted the steps and, standing beside his
daughter, said in a loud voice, "Whomever the Elephant
chooses, to him will my daughter be given in marriage."

The Princess Turquoise watched the clumsy, uncouth
creature led into the circle that had been formed by her
suitors, her eyes filled with an expression of fear and of
dread. In a few moments her fate would be decided for
her. The Elephant was lifting its thick, heavy trunk,
waving it backwards and forwards in all directions like
a great tentacle stretching out and feeling for guidance
in the air, and then suddenly he folded his trunk inwards,
threw it out again, broke the circle, crashed through the
crowds scattering them wide, wound his trunk round
the waist of a boy, and swiftly lifted him on high and
very gently deposited him at the feet of the Princess.

A roar of horror broke from the crowd: "The Elephant has chosen a beggar."

"It is a mistake," thundered the King, too thunder-struck to give himself time to think of what he was saying.

A hush fell over the assembly. The King had dared to say the Elephant was mistaken. Such a thing had never been heard of, for the Elephant was guided by the gods and was known to be sacred. The Princess Turquoise rose from her seat and said, "As the Elephant has decreed so it will be," and stretched out both her arms to the beggar boy, who was no other than the goat-herd.

The King ordered the goat-herd to be dragged away. "The Elephant's choice is my own," wailed the Princess, wringing her hands. "Dirty or ragged, I will have him for my husband."

"I would rather see you unwed," said the King. "It is a terrible mistake. The Elephant must choose once more."

Again the circle was formed, and again, this time without a moment's hesitation, the Elephant plunged into the crowd and pulled out the same boy.

Now the rejected princes turned on the boy and forced him back, but the Elephant followed after him, and his massive trunk lifted the boy out of their reach and for the third time set him before the Princess. Three times the Elephant had chosen, and the King knew there was nothing further to be done, so he turned to the Princess and said, "Take the beggar and be gone. This calamity has befallen us as a punishment for your willfulness."

But the people said nothing, for they saw plainly enough that love and happiness shone from the Princess's eyes, and they made a way for her to pass with her humble lover. That very night the Princess and her goat-herd were wed, and the bride's parents, to mark their disapproval, gave her for a dowry a lame horse, a blind donkey, and a cow without a horn.

After many hardships the Princess Turquoise and her husband managed to make their way back to the old Queen, who welcomed her son and his beautiful young wife. Amid great rejoicings the estates were given to them. The lame horse, the blind donkey, and the cow without a horn were returned to the Princess Turquoise's parents, together with many sacks of gold and a long letter telling them the story from beginning to end. When the King and Queen received these and learned how the wicked servant had betrayed his master, they sent their soldiers out to search for him. He was found and punished as he richly deserved. The innkeeper was rewarded handsomely, and to this very day he will tell you of a prince who once tended his goats.

It was not long before the King and Queen set off to their son-in-law's kingdom humbly to beg his forgiveness, which he readily consented to give. And the Princess Turquoise, who had proved so truly that she could be simple and yet queenly, lived happily with her handsome husband forever afterwards.

7

ALADDIN AND THE WONDERFUL LAMP

"AS IT WAS DIRTY SHE BEGAN TO RUB IT, THAT
IT MIGHT FETCH A HIGHER PRICE. INSTANTLY
A HIDEOUS GENIE APPEARED, AND ASKED WHAT
SHE WOULD HAVE."

There once lived a poor tailor, who had a son called Aladdin, a careless, idle boy who would do nothing but play all day long in the streets with little idle boys like himself. This so grieved the father that he died; yet, in spite of his mother's tears and prayers, Aladdin did not mend his ways. One day, when he was playing in the streets as usual, a stranger asked him his age, and if he was not the son of Mustapha the tailor.

"I am, sir," replied Aladdin; "but he died a long while ago."

On this the stranger, who was a famous African magician, fell on his neck and kissed him, saying: "I am your uncle, and knew you from your likeness to my brother. Go to your mother and tell her I am coming."

Aladdin ran home and told his mother of his newly found uncle.

"Indeed, child," she said, "your father had a brother, but I always thought he was dead."

However, she prepared supper, and bade Aladdin seek his uncle, who came laden with wine and fruit. He presently fell down and kissed the place where Mustapha used to sit, bidding Aladdin's mother not to be surprised at not having seen him before, as he had been forty years out of the country. He then turned to Aladdin, and asked him his trade, at which the boy hung his head, while his mother burst into tears. On learning that Aladdin was idle and would learn no trade, he offered to take a shop for him and stock it with merchandise. Next day he bought Aladdin a fine suit of clothes and took him all over the city, showing him the sights, and brought him home at nightfall to his mother, who was overjoyed to see her son so fine.

Next day the magician led Aladdin into some beautiful gardens a long way outside the city gates. They sat down by a fountain and the magician pulled a cake from his girdle, which he divided between them. They then journeyed onwards till they almost reached the mountains. Aladdin was so tired that he begged to go back, but the magician beguiled him with pleasant stories, and led him on in spite of himself. At last they came to two mountains divided by a narrow valley.

"We will go no further," said the false uncle. "I will show you something wonderful; only do you gather up sticks while I kindle a fire."

When it was lit the magician threw on it a powder he had about him, at the same time saying some magical words. The earth trembled a little and opened in front of them, disclosing a square flat stone with a brass ring in the middle to raise it by. Aladdin tried to run away, but the magician caught him and gave him a blow that knocked him down.

"What have I done, uncle?" he said piteously; whereupon the magician said more kindly:

"Fear nothing, but obey me. Beneath this stone lies a treasure which is to be yours, and no one else may touch it, so you must do exactly as I tell you."

At the word treasure Aladdin forgot his fears, and grasped the ring as he was told, saying the names of his father and grandfather. The stone came up quite easily, and some steps appeared.

"Go down," said the magician; "at the foot of those steps you will find an open door leading into three large halls. Tuck up your gown and go through them without touching anything, or you will die instantly. These halls lead into a garden of fine fruit trees. Walk on till you come to a niche in a terrace where stands a lighted lamp. Pour out the oil it contains, and bring it me."

He drew a ring from his finger and gave it to Aladdin, bidding him prosper.

Aladdin found everything as the magician had said, gathered some fruit off the trees, and, having got the lamp, arrived at the mouth of the cave. The magician cried out in a great hurry:

"Make haste and give me the lamp."

This Aladdin refused to do until he was out of the cave. The magician flew into a terrible passion, and throwing some more powder on to the fire, he said something, and the stone rolled back into its place.

The magician left Persia for ever, which plainly

showed that he was no uncle of Aladdin's, but a cunning magician, who had read in his magic books of a wonderful lamp, which would make him the most powerful man in the world. Though he alone knew where to find it, he could only receive it from the hand of another. He had picked out the foolish Aladdin for this purpose, intending to get the lamp and kill him afterwards.

For two days Aladdin remained in the dark, crying and lamenting. At last he clasped his hands in prayer, and in so doing rubbed the ring, which the magician had forgotten to take from him. Immediately an enormous and frightful genie rose out of the earth, saying:

"What wouldst thou with me? I am the Slave of the Ring, and will obey thee in all things."

Aladdin fearlessly replied: "Deliver me from this place!" whereupon the earth opened, and he found himself outside. As soon as his eyes could bear the light he went home, but fainted on the threshold. When he came to himself he told his mother what had passed, and showed her the lamp and the fruits he had gathered in the garden, which were in reality precious stones. He then asked for some food.

"Alas! child," she said, "I have nothing in the house, but I have spun a little cotton and will go and sell it."

Aladdin bade her keep her cotton, for he would sell the lamp instead. As it was very dirty she began to rub it, that it might fetch a higher price. Instantly a hideous genie appeared, and asked what she would have. She fainted away, but Aladdin, snatching the lamp, said boldly:

"Fetch me something to eat!"

The genie returned with a silver bowl, twelve silver

plates containing rich meats, two silver cups, and two bottles of wine. Aladdin's mother, when she came to herself, said:

"Whence comes this splendid feast?"

"Ask not, but eat," replied Aladdin. So they sat at breakfast till it was dinner-time, and Aladdin told his mother about the lamp. She begged him to sell it, and have nothing to do with devils.

"No," said Aladdin, "since chance hath made us aware of its virtues, we will use it, and the ring likewise, which I shall always wear on my finger." When they had eaten all the genie had brought Aladdin sold one of the silver plates, and so on until none was left. He then had recourse to the genie, who gave him another set of plates, and thus they lived for many years.

One day Aladdin heard an order from the Sultan proclaiming that everyone was to stay at home and close his

shutters while the Princess, his daughter, went to and from the bath. Aladdin was seized by a desire to see her face, which was very difficult, as she always went veiled. He hid himself behind the door of the bath, and peeped through a chink. The Princess lifted her veil as she went in, and looked so beautiful that Aladdin fell in love with her at first sight. He went home so changed that his mother was frightened. He told her he loved the Princess so deeply that he could not live without her, and meant to ask her in marriage of her father. His mother, on hearing this, burst out laughing, but Aladdin at last prevailed upon her to go before the Sultan and carry his request. She fetched a napkin and laid in it the magic fruits from the enchanted garden, which sparkled and shone like the most beautiful jewels. She took these with her to please the Sultan, and set out, trusting in the lamp. The Grand Vizier and the lords of council had just gone in as she entered the hall and placed herself in front of the Sultan. He, however, took no notice of her. She went every day for a week, and stood in the same place. When the council broke up on the sixth day the Sultan said to his Vizier:

"I see a certain woman in the audience-chamber every day carrying something in a napkin. Call her next time, that I may find out what she wants."

Next day, at a sign from the Vizier, she went up to the foot of the throne and remained kneeling till the Sultan said to her:

"Rise, good woman, and tell me what you want." She hesitated, so the Sultan sent away all but the Vizier, and bade her speak freely, promising to forgive her beforehand for anything she might say. She then told him of her son's violent love for the Princess.

"I prayed him to forget her," she said, "but in vain; he

threatened to do some desperate deed if I refused to go and ask your Majesty for the hand of the Princess. Now I pray you to forgive not me alone, but my son Aladdin."

The Sultan asked her kindly what she had in the napkin, whereupon she unfolded the jewels and presented them. He was thunderstruck, and turning to the Vizier said:

"What sayest thou? Ought I not to bestow the Princess on one who values her at such a price?"

The Vizier, who wanted her for his own son, begged the Sultan to withhold her for three months, in the course of which he hoped his son would contrive to make him a richer present. The Sultan granted this, told Aladdin's mother that, though he consented to the marriage, she must not appear before him again for three months.

Aladdin waited patiently for nearly three months, but after two had elapsed his mother, going into the city to buy oil, found every one rejoicing, and asked what was going on. "Do you not know," was the answer, "that the son of the Grand Vizier is to marry the Sultan's daughter to-night?" Breathless, she ran and told Aladdin, who was overwhelmed at first, but presently bethought him of the lamp. He rubbed it, and the genie appeared, saying:

"What is thy will?"

Aladdin replied: "The Sultan, as thou knowest, has broken his promise to me, and the Vizier's son is to have the Princess. My command is that to-night you bring hither the bride and bridegroom."

"Master, I obey," said the genie.

Aladdin then went to his chamber, where, sure enough, at midnight the genie transported the bed containing the Vizier's son and the Princess. "Take this new-married man," he said, "and put him outside in the cold, and return at daybreak." Whereupon the genie took the Vizier's son out of bed, leaving Aladdin with the Princess.

"Fear nothing," Aladdin said to her; "you are my wife, promised to me by your unjust father, and no harm shall come to you."

The Princess was too frightened to speak, and passed the most miserable night of her life, while Aladdin lay down beside her and slept soundly. At the appointed hour the genie fetched in the shivering bridegroom, laid him in his place, and transported the bed back to the palace.

Presently the Sultan came to wish his daughter good-morning. The unhappy Vizier's son jumped up and hid himself, while the Princess would not say a word, and was very sorrowful. The Sultan sent her mother to her, who said: "How comes it, child, that you will not speak to your father? What has happened?" The Princess sighed deeply, and at last told her mother how, during the night, the bed had been carried into some strange house, and what had passed there. Her mother did not believe her in the least, but bade her rise and consider it an idle dream.

The following night exactly the same thing happened, and next morning, on the Princess's refusing to speak, the Sultan threatened to cut off her head. She then confessed all, bidding him ask the Vizier's son if it were not so. The Sultan told the Vizier to ask his son, who owned the truth, adding that, dearly as he loved the Princess, he had rather die than go through another such fearful night, and wished to be separated from her. His wish was granted, and there was an end of feasting and rejoicing.

When the three months were over, Aladdin sent his mother to remind the Sultan of his promise. She stood in the same place as before, and the Sultan, who had forgotten Aladdin, at once remembered him, and sent for her. On seeing her poverty the Sultan felt less inclined than ever to keep his word, and asked his Vizier's advice, who counselled him to set so high a value on the Princess that no man living could come up to it. The Sultan then turned to Aladdin's mother, saying:

"Good woman, a sultan must remember his promises, and I will remember mine, but your son must first send me forty basins of gold brimful of jewels, carried by forty black slaves, led by as many white ones, splendidly dressed. Tell him that I await his answer."

The mother of Aladdin bowed low and went home, thinking all was lost. She gave Aladdin the message, adding:

"He may wait long enough for your answer!"

"Not so long, mother, as you think," her son replied. "I would do a great deal more than that for the Princess."

He summoned the genie, and in a few moments the eighty slaves arrived, and filled up the small house and garden. Aladdin made them set out to the palace, two and two, followed by his mother. They were so richly dressed, with such splendid jewels in their girdles, that everyone crowded to see them and the basins of gold they carried on their heads. They entered the palace, and, after kneeling before the Sultan, stood in a half-circle round the throne with their arms crossed, while Aladdin's mother presented them to the Sultan. He hesitated no longer, but said:

"Good woman, return and tell your son that I wait for him with open arms." She lost no time in telling Aladdin, bidding him make haste. But Aladdin first called the genie.

"I want a scented bath," he said, "a richly embroidered habit, a horse surpassing the Sultan's, and twenty slaves to attend me. Besides this, six slaves, beautifully dressed, to wait on my mother; and lastly, ten thousand pieces of gold in ten purses."

No sooner said than done. Aladdin mounted his horse and passed through the streets, the slaves strewing gold as they went. Those who had played with him in his childhood knew him not, he had grown so handsome. When the Sultan saw him he came down from his throne, embraced him, and led him into a hall where a feast was spread, intending to marry him to the Princess that very day. But Aladdin refused, saying, "I must build a palace fit for her," and took his leave. Once home, he said to the genie:

"Build me a palace of the finest marble, set with jasper, agate, and other precious stones. In the middle you shall build me a large hall with a dome, its four walls of massy gold and silver, each side having six windows, whose lattices, all except one which is to be left unfinished, must be set with diamonds and rubies. There must be stables and horses and grooms and slaves; go and see about it!"

The palace was finished by next day, and the genie carried him there and showed him all his orders faithfully carried out, even to the laying of a velvet carpet from Aladdin's palace to the Sultan's. Aladdin's mother then dressed herself carefully, and walked to the palace with her slaves, while he followed her on horseback. The Sultan sent musicians with trumpets and cymbals to meet them, so that the air resounded with music and cheers. She was taken to the Princess, who saluted her and

treated her with great honor. At night the Princess said
good-bye to her father, and set out on the carpet for
Aladdin's palace, with his mother at her side, and followed by the hundred slaves. She was charmed at the
sight of Aladdin, who ran to receive her.

"Princess," he said, "blame your beauty for my bold-
ness if I have displeased you."

She told him that, having seen him, she willingly
obeyed her father in this matter. After the wedding had
taken place Aladdin led her into the hall, where a feast
was spread, and she supped with him, after which they
danced till midnight.

Next day Aladdin invited the Sultan to see the palace.
On entering the hall with the four-and-twenty windows,
with their rubies, diamonds, and emeralds, he cried:

"It is a world's wonder! There is only one thing that
surprises me. Was it by accident that one window was
left unfinished?"

"No, sir, by design," returned Aladdin. "I wished your
Majesty to have the glory of finishing this palace."

The Sultan was pleased, and sent for the best jewellers
in the city. He showed them the unfinished window, and
bade them fit it up like the others. "Sir," replied their
spokesman, "we cannot find jewels enough." The Sultan
had his own fetched, which they soon used, but to no
purpose, for in a month's time the work was not half
done. Aladdin, knowing that their task was vain, bade
them undo their work and carry the jewels back, and the
genie finished the window at his command. The Sultan
was surprised to receive his jewels again, and visited
Aladdin, who showed him the window finished. The Sultan embraced him, the envious Vizier meanwhile hinting
that it was the work of enchantment.

Aladdin had won the hearts of the people by his gentle bearing. He was made captain of the Sultan's armies, and won several battles for him, but remained modest and courteous as before, and lived thus in peace and content for several years.

But far away in Africa the magician remembered Aladdin, and by his magic arts discovered that Aladdin, instead of perishing miserably in the cave, had escaped, and had married a princess, with whom he was living in great honor and wealth. He knew that the poor tailor's son could only have accomplished this by means of the lamp, and travelled night and day till he reached the capital of China, bent on Aladdin's ruin. As he passed through the town he heard people talking everywhere about a marvellous palace.

"Forgive my ignorance," he asked, "what is this palace you speak of?"

"Have you not heard of Prince Aladdin's palace," was the reply, "the greatest wonder of the world? I will direct you if you have a mind to see it."

The magician thanked him who spoke, and having seen the palace knew that it had been raised by the Genie of the Lamp, and became half mad with rage. He determined to get hold of the lamp, and again plunge Aladdin into the deepest poverty.

Unluckily, Aladdin had gone a-hunting for eight days, which gave the magician plenty of time. He bought a dozen copper lamps, put them into a basket, and went to the palace, crying, "New lamps for old!" followed by a jeering crowd. The Princess, sitting in the hall of four-and-twenty windows, sent a slave to find out what the noise was about, who came back laughing, so that the Princess scolded her.

"Madam," replied the slave, "who can help laughing to see an old fool offering to exchange fine new lamps for old ones?" Another slave, hearing this, said: "There is an old one on the cornice there which he can have."

Now this was the magic lamp, which Aladdin had left there, as he could not take it out hunting with him. The Princess, not knowing its value, laughingly bade the slave to take it and make the exchange. She went and said to the magician: "Give me a new lamp for this." He snatched it and bade the slave take her choice, amid the jeers of the crowd. Little he cared, but left off crying his lamps, and went out of the city gates to a lonely place, where he remained till nightfall, when he pulled out the lamp and rubbed it. The genie appeared, and at the magician's command carried him, together with the palace and the Princess in it, to a lonely place in Africa.

Next morning the Sultan looked out of the window towards Aladdin's palace and rubbed his eyes, for it was gone. He sent for the Vizier and asked what had become of the palace. The Vizier looked out too, and was lost in astonishment. He again put it down to enchantment, and this time the Sultan believed him, and sent thirty men on horseback to fetch Aladdin in chains. They met him riding home, bound him, and forced him to go with them on foot. The people, however, who loved him, followed, armed, to see that he came to no harm. He was carried before the Sultan, who ordered the executioner to cut off his head. The executioner made Aladdin kneel down, bandaged his eyes, and raised his scimitar to strike. At that instant the Vizier, who saw that the crowd had forced their way into the courtyard and were scaling the walls to rescue Aladdin, called to the executioner to stay his hand. The people, indeed, looked so threatening that the Sultan gave way and ordered Aladdin to be unbound, and pardoned him in the sight of the crowd. Aladdin now begged to know what he had done.

"False wretch!" said the Sultan, "come hither," and showed him from the window the place where his palace had stood.

Aladdin was so amazed that he could not say a word.

"Where is my palace and my daughter?" demanded the Sultan. "For the first I am not so deeply concerned, but my daughter I must have, and you must find her or lose your head."

Aladdin begged for forty days in which to find her, promising if he failed to return and suffer death at the Sultan's pleasure. His prayer was granted, and he went forth sadly from the Sultan's presence. For three days he wandered about like a madman, asking everyone what had become of his palace, but they only laughed and pitied him. He came to the banks of a river, and knelt down to say his prayers before throwing himself in. In so doing he rubbed the magic ring he still wore. The genie he had seen in the cave appeared, and asked his will.

"Save my life, genie," said Aladdin, "and bring my palace back."

"That is not in my power," said the genie; "I am only the Slave of the Ring; you must ask him of the lamp."

"Even so," said Aladdin, "but thou canst take me to the palace, and set me down under my dear wife's window."

He at once found himself in Africa, under the window of the Princess, and fell asleep out of sheer weariness. He was awakened by the singing of the birds, and his heart was lighter. He saw plainly that all his misfortunes

were owing to the loss of the lamp, and vainly wondered
who had robbed him of it.

That morning the Princess rose earlier than she had
done since she had been carried into Africa by the magician, whose company she was forced to endure once
a day. She, however, treated him so harshly that he dared
not live there altogether. As she was dressing, one of her
women looked out and saw Aladdin. The Princess ran
and opened the window, and at the noise she made
Aladdin looked up. She called to him to come to her,
and great was the joy of these lovers at seeing each other
again. After he had kissed her Aladdin said:

"I beg of you, Princess, in God's name, before we speak
of anything else, for your own sake and mine, tell me
what has become of an old lamp I left on the cornice in
the hall of four-and-twenty windows, when I went
a-hunting."

"Alas!" she said, "I am the innocent cause of our sor-
rows," and told him of the exchange of the lamp.

"Now I know," cried Aladdin, "that we have to thank
the African magician for this! Where is the lamp?"

"He carries it about with him," said the Princess. "I
know, for he pulled it out of his breast to show me. He
wishes me to break my faith with you and marry him,
saying that you were beheaded by my father's command.
He is for ever speaking ill of you, but I only reply by my
tears. If I persist, I doubt not but he will use violence."
Aladdin comforted her, and left her for a while. He
changed clothes with the first person he met in the town,
and having bought a certain powder returned to the
Princess, who let him in by a little side door.

"Put on your most beautiful dress," he said to her, "and
receive the magician with smiles, leading him to believe

that you have forgotten me. Invite him to sup with you, and say you wish to taste the wine of his country. He will go for some and while he is gone I will tell you what to do."

She listened carefully to Aladdin and when he left her arrayed herself gaily for the first time since she left China. She put on a girdle and head-dress of diamonds, and, seeing in a glass that she was more beautiful than ever, received the magician, saying, to his great amazement:

"I have made up my mind that Aladdin is dead, and that all my tears will not bring him back to me, so I am resolved to mourn no more, and have therefore invited you to sup with me; but I am tired of the wines of China, and would fain taste those of Africa."

The magician flew to his cellar, and the Princess put the powder Aladdin had given her in her cup. When he returned she asked him to drink her health in the wine of Africa, handing him her cup in exchange for his, as a sign she was reconciled to him. Before drinking the magician made her a speech in praise of her beauty, but the Princess cut him short, saying:

"Let us drink first, and you shall say what you will afterwards."

She set her cup to her lips and kept it there, while the magician drained his to the dregs and fell back lifeless. The Princess then opened the door to Aladdin, and flung her arms round his neck; but Aladdin put her away, bidding her leave him, as he had more to do. He then went to the dead magician, took the lamp out of his vest, and bade the genie carry the palace and all in it back to China. This was done, and the Princess in her chamber only felt

two little shocks, and little thought she was at home
again.

The Sultan, who was sitting in his closet, mourning
for his lost daughter, happened to look up, and rubbed
his eyes, for there stood the palace as before! He hastened
thither, and Aladdin received him in the hall of the four-
and-twenty windows, with the Princess at his side. Aladdin told him what had happened, and showed him the
dead body of the magician, that he might believe. A ten
days' feast was proclaimed, and it seemed as if Aladdin
might now live the rest of his life in peace; but it was not
to be.

The African magician had a younger brother, who was,
if possible, more wicked and more cunning than himself.
He travelled to China to avenge his brother's death, and
went to visit a pious woman called Fatima, thinking she
might be of use to him. He entered her cell and clapped
a dagger to her breast, telling her to rise and do his bidding on pain of death. He changed clothes with her,
colored his face like hers, put on her veil, and murdered
her, that she might tell no tales. Then he went towards
the palace of Aladdin, and all the people, thinking he was
the holy woman, gathered round him, kissing his hands
and begging his blessing.

When he got to the palace there was such a noise going
on round him that the Princess bade her slave look out
of the window and ask what was the matter. The slave
said it was the holy woman, curing people by her touch
of their ailments, whereupon the Princess, who had long
desired to see Fatima, sent for her. On coming to the
Princess the magician offered up a prayer for her health
and prosperity. When he had done the Princess made

him sit by her, and begged him to stay with her always. The false Fatima, who wished for nothing better, consented, but kept his veil down for fear of discovery. The Princess showed him the hall, and asked him what he thought of it.

"It is truly beautiful," said the false Fatima. "In my mind it wants but one thing."

"And what is that?" said the Princess.

"If only a roc's egg," replied he, "were hung up from the middle of this dome, it would be the wonder of the world."

After this the Princess could think of nothing but the roc's egg, and when Aladdin returned from hunting he found her in a very ill humor. He begged to know what was amiss, and she told him that all her pleasure in the hall was spoilt for the want of a roc's egg hanging from the dome.

"If that is all," replied Aladdin, "you shall soon be happy."

He left her and rubbed the lamp, and when the genie appeared commanded him to bring a roc's egg. The genie gave such a loud and terrible shriek that the hall shook.

"Wretch!" he cried, "it is not enough that I have done everything for you, but you must command me to bring my master and hang him up in the midst of this dome? You and your wife and your palace deserve to be burnt to ashes, but that this request does not come from you, but from the brother of the African magician, whom you destroyed. He is now in your palace disguised as the holy woman—whom he murdered. He it was who put that wish into your wife's head. Take care of yourself, for he means to kill you." So saying, the genie disappeared.

Aladdin went back to the Princess, saying his head

ached, and requesting that the holy Fatima should be fetched to lay her hands on it. But when the magician came near, Aladdin, seizing his dagger, pierced him to the heart.

"What have you done?" cried the Princess. "You have killed the holy woman!"

"Not so," replied Aladdin, "but a wicked magician," and told her of how she had been deceived.

After this Aladdin and his wife lived in peace. He succeeded the Sultan when he died, and reigned for many years, leaving behind him a long line of kings.

8

VALIANT VICKY, THE BRAVE WEAVER

"IT IS EASY ENOUGH TO SHOOT A GREAT HULK-
ING MAN—THERE IS SOMETHING TO SEE,
SOMETHING TO AIM AT . . . BUT TO SHOOT
A *mosquito* WITH A *shuttle* IS QUITE AN-
OTHER THING."

Once upon a time there lived a little weaver, by name Victor Prince, but because his head was big, his legs thin, and he was altogether small, and weak, and ridiculous, his neighbors called him Vicky—Little Vicky the Weaver.

But despite his size, his thin legs, and his ridiculous appearance, Vicky was very valiant, and loved to *talk* for hours of his bravery, and the heroic acts he would perform if Fate gave him an opportunity. Only Fate did not, and in consequence Vicky remained Little Vicky the valiant weaver, who was laughed at by all for his boasting.

Now one day, as Vicky was sitting at his loom, weaving, a mosquito settled on his left hand just as he was throwing the shuttle from his right hand, and by chance, after gliding swiftly through the warp, the shuttle came flying into his left hand on the very spot where the mosquito had settled, and squashed it. Seeing this, Vicky became desperately excited: "It is as I have always said," he cried; "if I only had the chance I knew I could show my mettle! Now, I'd like to know how many people could have done that? Killing a mosquito is easy, and throwing a shuttle is easy, but to do both at one time is a mighty different affair! It is easy enough to shoot a great hulking man—there is something to see, something to aim at; then guns and crossbows are made for shooting; but to shoot a *mosquito* with a *shuttle* is quite another thing. That requires a man!"

The more he thought over the matter, the more elated he became over his skill and bravery, until he determined that he would no longer suffer himself to be called "Vicky." No! now that he had shown his mettle he would be called "Victor"—"Victor Prince"—or better still, "Prince Victor"; that was a name worthy his merits. But when he announced this determination to the neighbors, they roared with laughter, and though some did call him Prince Victor, it was with such sniggering and giggling and mock reverence that the little man flew home in a rage. Here he met with no better reception, for his wife, a fine handsome young woman, who was tired to death by her ridiculous little husband's whims and fancies, sharply bade him hold his tongue and not make a fool of himself. Upon this, beside himself with pride and mortification, he seized her by the hair, and beat her most unmercifully. Then, resolving to stay no longer in

a town where his merits were unrecognized, he bade her
prepare some bread for a journey, and set about packing
his bundle.

"I will go into the world!" he said to himself. "The man
who can shoot a mosquito dead with a shuttle ought not
to hide his light under a bushel." So off he set, with his
bundle, his shuttle, and a loaf of bread tied up in a ker-
chief.

Now as he journeyed he came to a city where a dreadful elephant came daily to make a meal off the inhabitants. Many mighty warriors had gone against it, but
none had returned. On hearing this the valiant little
weaver thought to himself, "Now is my chance! A great
haystack of an elephant will be a fine mark to a man who
has shot a mosquito with a shuttle!" So he went to the
King, and announced that he proposed single-handed to
meet and slay the elephant. At first the King thought the
little man was mad, but as he persisted in his words, he
told him that he was free to try his luck if he chose to run
the risk; adding that many better men than he had failed.

Nevertheless, our brave weaver was nothing daunted;
he even refused to take either sword or bow, but strutted
out to meet the elephant armed only with his shuttle.

"It is a weapon I thoroughly understand, good people," he replied boastfully to those who urged him to
choose some more deadly arm, "and it has done its work
in its time, I can tell you!"

It was a beautiful sight to see little Vicky swaggering
out to meet his enemy, while the townsfolk flocked to the
walls to witness the fight. Never was there such a valiant
weaver till the elephant, descrying its tiny antagonist,
trumpeted fiercely, and charged right at him, and then,
alas! all the little man's courage disappeared, and for-

getting his new name of Prince Victor he dropped his
bundle, his shuttle, and his bread, and bolted away as
fast as Vicky's legs could carry him.

Now it so happened that his wife had made the bread
ever so sweet, and had put all sorts of tasty spices in it,
because she wanted to hide the flavor of the poison she
had put in it also; for she was a wicked, revengeful
woman, who wanted to be rid of her tiresome, whimsical
little husband. And so, as the elephant charged past, it
smelt the delicious spices, and catching up the bread
with its long trunk, gobbled it up without stopping an
instant. Meanwhile fear lent speed to Vicky's short legs,
but though he ran like a hare, the elephant soon overtook
him. In vain he doubled and doubled, and the beast's
hot breath was on him, when in sheer desperation he
turned, hoping to bolt through the enormous creature's
legs; being half blind with fear, however, he ran full tilt
against them instead. Now, as luck would have it, at that
very moment the poison took effect, and the elephant
fell to the ground stone dead.

When the spectators saw the monster fall they could
scarcely believe their eyes, but their astonishment was
greater still when, running up to the scene of action, they
found Valiant Vicky seated in triumph on the elephant's
head, calmly mopping his face with his handkerchief.

"I had to pretend to run away," he explained, "or the
coward would never have engaged me. Then I gave him
a little push, and he fell down, as you see. Elephants are
big beasts, but they have no strength to speak of."

The good folks were amazed at the careless way in
which Valiant Vicky spoke of his achievement, and as
they had been too far off to see very distinctly what had
occurred, they went and told the King that the little

weaver was just a fearful wee man, and had knocked over
the elephant like a ninepin. Then the King said to himself, "None of my warriors and wrestlers, no, not even
the heroes of old, could have done this. I must secure
this little man's services if I can." So he asked Vicky why
he was wandering about the world.

"For pleasure, for service, or for conquest!" returned
Valiant Vicky, laying such stress on the last word that
the King, in a great hurry, made him Commander-in-
Chief of his whole army, for fear he should take service
elsewhere.

So there was Valiant Vicky a mighty fine warrior, and
as proud as a peacock of having fulfilled his own pre-
dictions.

"I knew it!" he would say to himself when he was
dressed out in full fig, with shining armor and waving
plumes, and spears, swords, and shields; "I *felt* I had it
in me!"

Now after some time a terribly savage tiger came rav-
aging the country, and at last the cityfolk petitioned that
the mighty Prince Victor might be sent out to destroy it.
So out he went at the head of his army—for he was a great
man now, and had quite forgotten all about looms and
shuttles. But first he made the King promise his daughter

HENRY
C PITZ

in marriage as a reward. "Nothing for nothing!" said the astute little weaver to himself, and when the promise was given he went out as gay as a lark.

"Do not distress yourselves, good people," he said to those who flocked round him praying for his successful return; "it is ridiculous to suppose the tiger will have a chance. Why, I knocked over an elephant with my little finger! I am really invincible!"

But, alas for our Valiant Vicky! No sooner did he see the tiger lashing its tail and charging down on him, than he ran for the nearest tree, and scrambled into the branches. There he sat like a monkey, while the tiger glowered at him from below. Of course when the army saw their Commander-in-Chief bolt like a mouse, they followed his example, and never stopped until they reached the city, where they spread the news that the little hero had fled up a tree.

"There let him stay!" said the King, secretly relieved, for he was jealous of the little weaver's prowess, and did not want him for a son-in-law.

Meanwhile, Valiant Vicky sat cowering in the tree, while the tiger occupied itself below with sharpening its teeth and claws, and curling its whiskers, till poor Vicky nearly tumbled into its jaws with fright. So one day, two days, three days, six days passed by; on the seventh the tiger was fiercer, hungrier, and more watchful than ever. As for the poor little weaver, he was so hungry that his hunger made him brave, and he determined to try and slip past his enemy during its midday snooze. He crept stealthily down inch by inch, till his foot was within a yard of the ground, and then? Why then the tiger, which had had one eye open all the time, jumped up with a roar!

Valiant Vicky shrieked with fear, and making a tremendous effort, swung himself into a branch, cocking his little bandy legs over it to keep them out of reach, for the tiger's red panting mouth and gleaming white teeth were within half an inch of his toes. In doing so, his dagger fell out of its sheath, and went pop into the tiger's wide-open mouth, and thus point foremost down into its stomach, so that it died!

Valiant Vicky could scarcely believe his good fortune, but, after prodding at the body with a branch, and finding it did not move, he concluded the tiger really was dead, and ventured down. Then he cut off its head, and went home in triumph to the King.

"You and your warriors are a nice set of cowards!" said he, wrathfully. "Here have I been fighting that tiger for seven days and seven nights, without bite or sup, whilst you have been guzzling and snoozing at home. Pah! it's disgusting! but I suppose every one is not a hero as I am!" So Prince Victor married the King's daughter, and was a greater man than ever.

But by and by a neighboring prince, who bore a grudge against the King, came with a huge army, and encamped outside the city, swearing to put every man, woman, and child within it to the sword. Hearing this, the inhabitants of course cried with one accord, "Prince Victor! Prince Victor to the rescue!" So the valiant little weaver was ordered by the King to go out and destroy the invading army, after which he was to receive half the kingdom as a reward. Now Valiant Vicky, with all his boasting, was no fool, and he said to himself, "This is a very different affair from the others. A man may kill a mosquito, an elephant, and a tiger; yet another man may kill *him*. And here is not one man, but thousands!

No, no!—What is the use of half a kingdom if you haven't a head on your shoulders? Under the circumstances I prefer *not* to be a hero!"

So in the dead of night he bade his wife rise, pack up her golden dishes, and follow him—"Not that you will want the golden dishes at my house," he explained boastfully, "for I have heaps and heaps, but on the journey these will be useful." Then he crept outside the city, followed by his wife carrying the bundle, and began to steal through the enemy's camp.

Just as they were in the very middle of it, a big cock-chafer flew into Valiant Vicky's face. "Run! run!" he shrieked to his wife, in a terrible taking, and setting off as fast as he could, never stopped till he had reached his room again and hidden under the bed. His wife set off at a run likewise, dropping her bundle of golden dishes with a clang. The noise roused the enemy, who, thinking they were attacked, flew to arms; but being half asleep, and the night being pitch-dark, they could not distinguish friend from foe, and falling on each other, fought with such fury that by next morning not one was left alive! And then, as may be imagined, great were the rejoicings at Prince Victor's prowess. "It was a mere trifle!" remarked that valiant little gentleman modestly; "when a man can shoot a mosquito with a shuttle, everything else is child's play."

So he received half the kingdom, and ruled it with great dignity, refusing ever afterwards to fight, saying truly that kings never fought themselves, but paid others to fight for them.

Thus he lived in peace, and when he died every one said Valiant Vicky was the greatest hero the world had ever seen.

9

THE DRAGON'S STRENGTH

"MY STRENGTH IS IN THE SPARROW. LET ANY-
ONE KILL THE SPARROW AND I SHOULD DIE
THAT INSTANT."

There was once a King who had three sons. One day the oldest son went hunting and when night fell his huntsmen came riding home without him.

"Where is the prince?" the King asked.

"Isn't he here?" the huntsmen said. "He left us in mid-afternoon chasing a hare near the Old Mill up the river. We haven't seen him since and we supposed he must have come home alone."

When he hadn't returned the following day his brother, the second prince, went out to search for him.

"I'll go to the Old Mill," he said to the King, "and see what's become of him."

So he mounted his horse and rode up the river. As he neared the Old Mill a hare crossed his path and the second prince being a hunter like his brother at once gave

[113]

chase. His attendant waited for his return but waited in vain. Night fell and still there was no sign of the second prince.

The attendant returned to the palace and told the King what had happened. The King was surprised but not unduly alarmed and the following day when the Youngest Prince asked to go hunting alone the King suggested that he go in the direction of the Old Mill to find out if he could what was keeping his brothers.

The Youngest Prince who had listened carefully to what his brothers' attendants had reported decided to act cautiously. So when a hare crossed his path as he approached the Old Mill, instead of giving it chase, he rode off as though he were hunting other game. Later he returned to the Old Mill from another direction.

He found an old woman sitting in front of it.

"Good evening, granny," he said in a friendly tone, pulling up his horse for a moment's chat. "Do you live here? You know I thought the Old Mill was deserted."

The old woman looked at him and shook her head gloomily.

"Deserted indeed! My boy, take an old woman's advice and don't have anything to do with this Old Mill! It's an evil place!"

"Why, granny," the Prince said, "what's the matter with it?"

The old woman peered cautiously around and when she saw they were alone she beckoned the Prince to come near. Then she whispered:

"A dragon lives here! A horrible monster! He takes the form of a hare and lures people into the mill. Then he captures them. Some of them he kills and eats and others he holds as prisoners in an underground dungeon.

I'm one of his prisoners and he keeps me here to work for him."

"Granny," the Youngest Prince said, "would you like me to rescue you?"

"My boy, you couldn't do it! You have no idea what a strong evil monster the dragon is."

"If you found out something for me, granny, I think I might be able to overcome the dragon and rescue you."

The old woman was doubtful but she promised to do anything the Youngest Prince asked.

"Well then, granny, find out from the dragon where his strength is, whether in his own body or somewhere else. Find out to-night and I'll come back to-morrow at this same hour to see you."

So that night when the dragon came home, after he had supped and when she was scratching his head to make him drowsy for bed, the old woman said to him:

"Master, I think you're the strongest dragon in the world! Tell me now, where does your strength lie—in your own beautiful body or somewhere else?"

"You're right, old woman," the dragon grunted: "I am pretty strong as dragons go. But I don't keep my strength in my own body. No, indeed! That would be too dangerous. I keep it in the hearth yonder."

At that the old woman ran over to the hearth and, stooping down, she kissed it and caressed it.

"O beautiful hearth!" she said, "where my master's strength is hidden! How happy are the ashes that cover your stones!"

The dragon laughed with amusement.

"That's the time I fooled you, old woman! My strength isn't in the hearth at all! It's in the tree in front of the mill."

The old woman at once ran out of the mill and threw her arms about the tree.

"O tree!" she cried, "most beautiful tree in the world, guard carefully our master's strength and let no harm come to it!"

Again the dragon laughed.

"I've fooled you another time, old woman! Come here and scratch my head some more and this time I'll tell you the truth for I see you really love your master."

So the old woman went back and scratched the dragon's head and the dragon told her the truth about his strength.

"I keep it far away," he said. "In the third kingdom from here near the Tsar's own city there is a deep lake. A dragon lives at the bottom of the lake. In the dragon there is a wild boar; in the boar a hare; in the hare a pigeon; in the pigeon a sparrow. My strength is in the sparrow. Let any one kill the sparrow and I should die that instant. But I am safe. No one but shepherds ever come to the lake and even they don't come any more for the dragon has eaten up so many of them that the lake has got a bad name. Indeed, nowadays even the Tsar himself is hard put to it to find a shepherd. Oh, I tell you, old woman, your master is a clever one!"

So now the old woman had the dragon's secret and the next day she told it to the Youngest Prince. He at once devised a plan whereby he hoped to overcome the dragon. He dressed himself as a shepherd and with crook in hand started off on foot for the third kingdom. He traveled through villages and towns, across rivers and over mountains, and reached at last the third kingdom and the Tsar's own city. He presented himself at the palace and asked employment as a shepherd.

The guards looked at him in surprise and said:

"A shepherd! Are you sure you want to be a shepherd?"

Then they called to their companions: "Here's a youth who wants to be a shepherd!" And the word went through the palace and even the Tsar heard it.

"Send the youth to me," he ordered.

"Do you really want to be my shepherd?" he asked the Youngest Prince.

The Youngest Prince said yes, he did.

"If I put you in charge of the sheep, where would you pasture them?"

"Isn't there a lake beyond the city," the Prince asked, "where the grazing is good?"

"H'm!" said the Tsar. "So you know about that lake, too! What else do you know?"

"I've heard the shepherds disappear."

"And still you want to try your luck?" the Tsar exclaimed.

Just then the Tsar's only daughter, a lovely Princess, who had been looking at the young stranger, slipped over to her father and whispered:

"But, father, you can't let such a handsome young man as that go off with the sheep! It would be dreadful if he never returned!"

The Tsar whispered back:

"Hush, child! Your concern for the young man's safety does credit to your noble feelings. But this is not the time or the place for sentiment. We must consider first the welfare of the royal sheep."

He turned to the Youngest Prince:

"Very well, young man, you may consider yourself engaged as shepherd. Provide yourself with whatever you need and assume your duties at once."

"There is one thing," the Youngest Prince said. "When I start out to-morrow morning with the sheep I should like to take with me two strong boarhounds, a falcon, and a set of bagpipes."

"You shall have them all," the Tsar promised.

Early the next morning when the Princess peeped out of her bedroom window she saw the new shepherd driving the royal flocks to pasture. A falcon was perched on his shoulder; he had a set of bagpipes under his arm; and he was leading two powerful boarhounds on a leash.

"It's a shame!" the Princess said to herself. "He'll probably never return and he's such a handsome young man, too!" And she was so unhappy at thought of never again seeing the new shepherd that she couldn't go back to sleep.

Well, the Youngest Prince reached the lake and turned out his sheep to graze. He perched the falcon on a log, tied the dogs beside it, and laid his bagpipes on the ground. Then he took off his smock, rolled up his hose, and wading boldly into the lake called out in a loud voice:

"Ho, dragon, come out and we'll try a wrestling match! That is, if you're not afraid!"

"Afraid?" bellowed an awful voice. "Who's afraid?"

The water of the lake churned this way and that and a horrible scaly monster came to the surface. He crawled out on shore and clutched the Prince around the waist. And the Prince clutched him in a grip just as strong and there they swayed back and forth, and rolled over, and wrestled together on the shore of the lake without either getting the better of the other. By midafternoon when the sun was hot, the dragon grew faint and cried out:

"Oh, if I could but dip my burning head in the cool water, then I could toss you as high as the sky!"

"Don't talk nonsense!" the Prince said. "If the Tsar's daughter would kiss my forehead, then I could toss you twice as high!"

After that the dragon slipped out of the Prince's grasp, plunged into the water, and disappeared. The Prince waited for him but he didn't show his scaly head again that day.

When evening came, the Prince washed off the grime of the fight, dressed himself carefully, and then looking as fresh and handsome as ever drove home his sheep. With the falcon on his shoulder and the two hounds at his heels he came playing a merry tune on his bagpipes.

The townspeople hearing the bagpipes ran out of their houses and cried to each other:

"The shepherd's come back!"

The Princess ran to her window and, when she saw the shepherd alive and well, she put her hand to her heart and said:

"Oh!"

Even the Tsar was pleased.

"I'm not a bit surprised that he's back!" he said. "There's something about this youth that I like!"

The next day the Tsar sent two of his trusted servants to the lake to see what was happening there. They hid themselves behind some bushes on a little hill that commanded the lake. They were there when the shepherd arrived and they watched him as he waded out into the water and challenged the dragon as on the day before.

They heard the shepherd call out in a loud voice:

"Ho, dragon, come out and we'll try a wrestling match! That is, if you're not afraid!"

And from the water they heard an awful voice bellow back:

"Afraid? Who's afraid?"

Then they saw the water of the lake churn this way and that and a horrible scaly monster come to the surface. They saw him crawl out on shore and clutch the shepherd around the waist. And they saw the shepherd clutch him in a grip just as strong. And they watched the two as they swayed back and forth and rolled over and wrestled together without either getting the better of the other. By midafternoon when the sun grew hot they saw the dragon grow faint and they heard him cry out:

"Oh, if I could only dip my burning head in the cool water, then I could toss you as high as the sky!"

And they heard the shepherd reply:

"Don't talk nonsense! If the Tsar's daughter would kiss my forehead, then I could toss you twice as high!"

Then they saw the dragon slip out of the shepherd's grasp, plunge into the water, and disappear. They waited but he didn't show his scaly head again that day.

So the Tsar's servants hurried home before the shepherd and told the Tsar all they had seen and heard. The Tsar was mightily impressed with the bravery of the shepherd and he declared that if he killed that horrid dragon he should have the Princess herself for wife!

He sent for his daughter and told her all that his servants had reported and he said to her:

"My daughter, you, too, can help rid your country of this monster if you go out with the shepherd to-morrow and when the time comes kiss him on the forehead. You will do this, will you not, for your country's sake?"

The Princess blushed and trembled and the Tsar, looking at her in surprise, said:

"What! Shall a humble shepherd face a dragon un-afraid and the daughter of the Tsar tremble!"

"Father," the Princess cried, "it isn't the dragon that I'm afraid of!"

"What then?" the Tsar asked.

But what it was she was afraid of the Princess would not confess. Instead she said:

"If the welfare of my country require that I kiss the shepherd on the forehead, I shall do so."

So the next morning when the shepherd started out with his sheep, the falcon on his shoulder, the dogs at his heels, the bagpipes under his arm, the Princess walked beside him.

Her eyes were downcast and he saw that she was trembling.

"Do not be afraid, dear Princess," he said to her. "Nothing shall harm you—I promise that!"

"I'm not afraid," the Princess murmured. But she continued to blush and tremble and, although the shepherd tried to look into her eyes to reassure her, she kept her head averted.

This time the Tsar himself and many of his courtiers had gone on before and taken their stand on the hill that overlooked the lake to see the final combat of the shepherd and the dragon.

When the shepherd and the Princess reached the lake, the shepherd put his falcon on the log as before and tied the dogs beside it and laid his bagpipes on the ground. Then he threw off his smock, rolled up his hose, and wading boldly into the lake called out in a loud voice:

"Ho, dragon, come out and we'll try a wrestling match! That is, if you're not afraid!"

"Afraid?" bellowed an awful voice. "Who's afraid?"

The water of the lake churned this way and that and the horrible scaly monster came to the surface. He crawled to shore and clutched the shepherd around the waist. The shepherd clutched him in a grip just as strong and there they swayed back and forth and rolled over and wrestled together on the shore of the lake without

either getting the better of the other. The Princess without the least show of fear stood nearby calling out encouragement to the shepherd and waiting for the moment when the shepherd should need her help.

By midafternoon when the sun was hot, the dragon grew faint and cried out:

"Oh, if I could but dip my burning head in the cool water, then I could toss you as high as the sky!"

"Don't talk nonsense!" the shepherd said. "If the Tsar's daughter would kiss my forehead then I could toss you twice as high!"

Instantly the Princess ran forward and kissed the shepherd three times. The first kiss fell on his forehead, the second on his nose, the third on his mouth. With each kiss his strength increased an hundredfold and taking the dragon in a mighty grip he tossed him up so high that for a moment the Tsar and all the courtiers lost sight of him in the sky. Then he fell to earth with such a thud that he burst.

Out of his body sprang a wild boar. The shepherd was ready for this and on the moment he unleashed the two hounds and they fell on the boar and tore him to pieces.

Out of the boar jumped a rabbit. It went leaping across the meadow but the dogs caught it and killed it.

Out of the rabbit flew a pigeon. Instantly the shepherd

unloosed the falcon. It rose high in the air, then swooped down upon the pigeon, clutched it in its talons, and delivered it into the shepherd's hands.

He cut open the pigeon and found the sparrow.

"Spare me! Spare me!" squawked the sparrow.

"Tell me where my brothers are," the shepherd demanded with his fingers about the sparrow's throat.

"Your brothers? They are alive and in the deep dungeon that lies below the Old Mill. Behind the mill there are three willow saplings growing from one old root. Cut the saplings and strike the root. A heavy iron door leading down into the dungeon will open. In the dungeon you will find many captives old and young, your brothers among them. Now that I have told you this are you going to spare my life?"

But the shepherd wrung the sparrow's neck for he knew that only in that way could the monster who had captured his brothers be killed.

Well, now that the dragon was dead the Tsar and all his courtiers came down from the hill and embraced the shepherd and told him what a brave youth he was.

"You have delivered us all from a horrid monster," the Tsar said, "and to show you my gratitude and the country's gratitude I offer you my daughter for wife."

"Thank you," said the shepherd, "but I couldn't think of marrying the Princess unless she is willing to marry me."

The Princess blushed and trembled just as she had blushed and trembled the night before and that morning, too, on the way to the lake. She tried to speak but could not at first. Then in a very little voice she said:

"As a Princess I think it is my duty to marry this brave shepherd who has delivered my country from this terrible dragon, and—and I think I should want to marry him anyway."

She said the last part of her speech in such a very low voice that only the shepherd himself heard it. But that was right enough because after all it was intended only for him.

So then and there beside the lake before even the shepherd had time to wash his face and hands and put on his smock the Tsar put the Princess's hand in his hand and pronounced them betrothed.

After that the shepherd bathed in the lake and then refreshed and clean he sounded his bagpipes and he and the Princess and the Tsar and all the courtiers returned to the city driving the sheep before them.

All the townspeople came out to meet them and they danced to the music of the bagpipes and there was great rejoicing both over the death of the dragon and over the betrothal of the Princess and the brave shepherd.

The wedding took place at once and the wedding festivities lasted a week. Such feasting as the townspeople had! Such music and dancing!

When the wedding festivities were ended, the shepherd told the Tsar who he really was.

"You say you're a Prince!" the Tsar cried, perfectly delighted at this news. Then he declared he wasn't in the least surprised. In fact, he said, he had suspected as much from the first!

"Do you think it likely," he asked somewhat pompously, "that any daughter of mine would fall in love with a man who wasn't a prince?"

"I think I'd have fallen in love with you whatever you were!" whispered the Princess to her young husband. But she didn't let her father hear her!

The Prince told the Tsar about his brothers' captivity and how he must go home to release them, and the Tsar at once said that he and his bride might go provided they returned as soon as possible.

They agreed to this and the Tsar fitted out a splendid escort for them and sent them away with his blessing.

So the Prince now traveled back through the towns and villages of three kingdoms, across rivers and over mountains, no longer a humble shepherd on foot, but a rich and mighty personage riding in a manner that befitted his rank.

When he reached the deserted mill, his friend the old woman was waiting for him.

"I know, my Prince, you have succeeded for the monster has disappeared."

"Yes, granny, you are right: I have succeeded. I found the dragon in the lake, and the boar in the dragon, and the rabbit in the boar, and the pigeon in the rabbit, and the sparrow in the pigeon. I took the sparrow and killed it. So you are free now, granny, to return to your home. And soon all those other poor captives will be free."

He went behind the mill and found the three willow saplings. He cut them off and struck the old root. Sure enough a heavy iron door opened. This led down into a deep dungeon which was crowded with unfortunate prisoners. The Prince led them all out and sent them their various ways. He found his own two brothers among them and led them home to his father.

There was great rejoicing in the King's house, and in the King's heart, too, for he had given up hope of ever seeing any of his sons again.

The King was so charmed with the Princess that he

said it was a pity that she couldn't marry his oldest son so that she might one day be Queen.

"The Youngest Prince is a capable young man," the King said, "and there's no denying that he managed this business of killing the dragon very neatly. But he is after all only the Youngest Prince with very little hope of succeeding to the kingdom. If you hadn't married him in such haste one of his older brothers might easily have fallen in love with you."

"I don't regret my haste," the Princess said. "Besides he is now my father's heir. But that doesn't matter for I should be happy with the Youngest Prince if he were only a shepherd."

10

STORY OF ALI BABA AND THE FORTY THIEVES

<><><><><><><><><><><><><><><><><><><><><><><><><><><><><><><><><><>

"ACCORDINGLY HE WENT AMONG THE SHRUBS
AND PERCEIVING THE DOOR CONCEALED BE-
HIND THEM, STOOD BEFORE IT, AND SAID,
'OPEN SESAME.' THE DOOR INSTANTLY FLEW
WIDE OPEN."

<><><><><><><><><><><><><><><><><><><><><><><><><><><><><><><><><><>

There lived in ancient times, in Persia, two brothers, one named Cassim, the other Ali Baba. Their father left them scarcely anything, but he divided the little property he had equally between them.

Cassim married a wife, who soon after became an heiress to a large sum, and a warehouse full of rich goods; so that he all at once became one of the wealthiest and most considerable merchants, and lived at his ease.

Ali Baba on the other hand, who had married a woman as poor as himself, lived in a very wretched habitation, and maintained his wife and children by cutting wood, which he carried to town upon his three asses, and there sold.

One day, when Ali Baba was in the forest, and had cut wood enough to load his asses, he saw at a distance a great cloud of dust, and soon he perceived a troop of horsemen coming towards him. Fearing that they might be thieves, he climbed into a large tree, whose branches were so thick that he was completely hidden. He placed himself in the middle of the tree, from whence he could see all that passed without being discovered. The tree stood at the base of a rock, so steep and craggy that nobody could climb up.

The troop of men, who were all well mounted, came to the foot of this rock, and there dismounted. Ali Baba counted forty of them, and, from their looks, was assured that they were thieves. Nor was he mistaken, for they were a band of robbers, who without doing any harm to the neighborhood, robbed at a distance. Every man unbridled his horse, tied him to a shrub, and hung about his neck a bag of corn. Then each of them took a wallet from his horse, which from its weight seemed to Ali Baba to be full of gold and silver. One who seemed to be the captain of the band, came, with his wallet upon his back, under the tree in which Ali Baba was concealed, and making his way through the shrubs, he stood before the rock, and pronounced distinctly these words: "Open Sesame." As soon as the captain of the robbers had uttered these words a door opened in the rock, and after he had made all his band enter before him, the captain followed, and the door shut again of itself.

The robbers stayed some time within the rock, and Ali Baba, who feared that one of them might come out

and catch him, if he should endeavor to make his escape, was obliged to sit patiently in the tree. At last the door opened again, and the forty robbers came out. The captain came first, and stood to see the others all pass by him, then he pronounced these words: "Shut Sesame," and instantly the door of the rock closed again as it was before. Every man bridled his horse, fastened his wallet, and mounted, and when the captain saw them ready, he put himself at their head, and they returned by the way they had come.

Ali Baba did not immediately quit his tree, but followed the band of robbers with his eyes as far as he could see them. He then descended, and remembering the words the robber captain had used to cause the door to open and shut, he was filled with curiosity to try if his pronouncing them would have the same effect. Accordingly he went among the shrubs, and perceiving the door concealed behind them, stood before it, and said: "Open Sesame." The door instantly flew wide open.

Ali Baba was surprised to find a cavern well lighted and spacious, in the form of a vault, which received the light from an opening at the top of the rock. He saw rich bales of silk stuff, brocade, and valuable carpeting, piled upon one another; gold and silver ingots in great heaps, and money in bags. The sight of all these riches made him suppose that this cave must have been occupied for ages by bands of robbers, who had succeeded one another.

Ali Baba immediately entered the cave, and as soon as he did so, the door shut of itself. This did not disturb him, because he knew the secret with which to open it again. He paid no attention to the silver, but carried out much of the gold coin, which was in bags. He collected his asses, which had strayed away, and when he had loaded them with the bags, laid wood over in such a manner, that the bags could not be seen. When he had done this he stood before the door, and pronounced the words: "Shut Sesame," and the door closed after him. He then made the best of his way to town.

When Ali Baba reached home, he drove his asses into a little yard, shut the gates very carefully, threw off the wood that covered the bags, and carried them into the house, and ranged them in order before his wife. He then emptied the bags, which raised such a heap of gold, as dazzled her eyes, and when he had done this he told her the whole adventure from beginning to end, and, above all, charged her to keep it secret.

Ali Baba found the heap of gold so large that it was im-

possible to count so much in one night; he therefore sent
his wife out to borrow a small measure in the neighborhood. Away she ran to her brother-in-law Cassim, who
lived near by, and asked his wife to lend her a measure
for a little while. The sister-in-law did so, but as she knew
Ali Baba's poverty, she was curious to discover what sort
of grain his wife wanted to measure, and she artfully put
some suet in the bottom of the measure.

Ali Baba's wife went home, and measured the heap of
gold, and carried the measure back again to her sister-in-
law, but without noticing that a piece had stuck to the
bottom. As soon as she was gone, Cassim's wife examined
the measure, and was inexpressibly surprised to find a
piece of gold stuck to it. Envy immediately possessed her
breast. "What!" said she, "has Ali Baba gold so plentiful
as to measure it? Where has that poor wretch got all his
wealth?" Cassim, her husband, was not at home, and she
waited for his return, with great impatience.

When Cassim came home, his wife said to him: "Cassim, I know that thou thinkest thyself rich, but thou art
mistaken. Ali Baba is infinitely richer than thou. He does
not count his money, but measures it!" Cassim desired
her to explain the riddle, which she did, by telling him of
the stratagem she had used to make the discovery, and
she showed him the piece of money, which was so old
that they could not tell in what prince's reign it had been
coined.

Cassim, instead of being pleased, conceived a base
envy of his brother's prosperity. He could not sleep all
that night, and in the morning went to him before sun-
rise. "Ali Baba," said he, showing him the piece of
money, which his wife had given him, "thou pretendest
to be miserably poor, and yet thou measurest gold! How

many of these pieces hast thou? My wife found this at the bottom of the measure thou borrowedest yesterday."

Ali Baba, perceiving that Cassim and his wife knew all, told his brother, without showing the least surprise or trouble, by what chance he had discovered this retreat of thieves. He told him also in what place it was, and offered him part of his treasure to keep the secret. "I expect as much," replied Cassim haughtily, "but I must know exactly where this treasure is, and how I may visit it myself when I choose; otherwise I will go and inform the Cadi, that thou hast this gold. Thou wilt then lose all thou hast, and I shall have a share for my information."

Ali Baba, more out of good nature, than because he was frightened by the insulting menaces of his unnatural brother, told him all he desired, and taught him the very words he was to use to gain admission into the cave. Cassim, who wanted no more of Ali Baba, left him, and immediately set out for the forest with ten mules bearing great chests, which he designed to fill with treasure. He followed the road which Ali Baba had pointed out to him, and it was not long before he reached the rock, and found out the place by the tree, and by the other marks which his brother had described.

When he discovered the entrance to the cave he pronounced the words: "Open Sesame." The door opened immediately, and when he had entered, closed upon him. In examining the cave, he found much more riches than he had imagined. He was so covetous, and greedy of wealth, that he could have spent the whole day feasting his eyes upon so much treasure, if the thought that he had come to carry away some had not hindered him.

He laid as many bags of gold as he could carry at the door of the cavern, but his thoughts were so full of the great riches he should possess, that he could not think of the words to make the door open, but instead of Sesame, said: "Open Barley," and was much amazed to find that the door remained fast shut. He named several sorts of grains, but still the door would not open, and the more he endeavored to remember the word Sesame, the more his memory was confounded. He threw down the bags he had loaded himself with, and walked distractedly up and down the cave, without the least regard to the riches that were around him.

About noon the robbers chanced to visit their cave, and at some distance saw Cassim's mules straggling about the rock, with great chests upon their backs. Alarmed at this the robbers galloped at full speed to the cave. They dismounted, and while some of them searched about the rock, the captain and the rest went directly to the door, with their naked sabres in their hands, and pronouncing the proper words it opened. Cassim, seeing the door open, rushed towards it in order to escape, but the robbers with their sabres soon deprived him of his life.

The first care of the robbers, after this, was to examine the cave. They found all the bags which Cassim had brought to the door to be ready to load his mules, and they carried them again to their places, without missing what Ali Baba had taken before. Then, holding a council, they deliberated on the occurrence. They could not imagine how Cassim had gained entrance into the cave, for they were all persuaded that nobody knew their secret, little thinking that Ali Baba had watched them. It was a matter of the greatest importance to them to secure their riches. They agreed, therefore, to cut Cassim's body into four quarters, to hang two on one side and two on the other, within the door of the cave, in order to terrify any person, who should attempt to enter. They had no sooner taken this resolution than they put it into execution. They then left the place, closed the door, mounted their horses, and departed to attack any caravans they might meet.

In the meantime, Cassim's wife was very uneasy when darkness approached, and her husband had not returned. She spent the night in tears, and when morning came she ran to Ali Baba in alarm. He did not wait for his sister-in-law to desire him to see what had become of Cassim, but departed immediately with his three asses, begging her first to moderate her anxiety.

He went to the forest, and when he came near the rock was seriously alarmed at finding some blood spilt near the door, but when he pronounced the words, "Open Sesame," and the door opened, he was struck with horror at the dismal sight of his brother's quarters. He entered the cave, took down the remains, and having loaded one of his asses with them, covered them over with wood. The other two asses he loaded with bags of gold, covering them with wood also as before, then bidding the door shut he left the cave. When he came home, he drove the two asses loaded with gold into his little yard, and left the care of unloading them to his wife, while he led the other to his sister-in-law's house.

Ali Baba knocked at the door, which was opened by Morgiana, an intelligent slave, whom Ali Baba knew to be faithful and resourceful in the most difficult undertakings. When he came into the court, he unloaded the ass, and taking Morgiana aside, said to her: "The first thing I ask of thee is inviolable secrecy, which thou wilt find is necessary both for thy mistress's sake and mine. Thy master's body is contained in these two bundles, and our business is to bury him as though he had died a natural death. Go tell thy mistress that I wish to speak to her, and mind what I have said to thee."

Morgiana went to her mistress and Ali Baba followed her. Ali Baba then detailed the incidents of his journey, and of Cassim's death. He endeavored to comfort the widow, and said to her: "I offer to add the treasures which Allah hath sent me, to what thou hast, and marry thee, assuring thee that my wife will not be jealous, and that we shall be happy together. If this proposal is agreeable to thee, I think that thou mayest leave the management of Cassim's funeral to Morgiana, the faithful slave, and I will contribute all that lies in my power to thy consolation."

What could Cassim's widow do better than accept this proposal? She therefore dried her tears, which had begun to flow abundantly, and showed Ali Baba that she approved of his proposal. He then left the widow, recommended Morgiana to care for her master's body, and returned home with his ass.

The next morning, soon after day appeared, Morgiana, knowing an old cobbler who opened his stall early, went to him and bidding him good-morrow, put a piece of gold into his hand. "Well," said Baba Mustapha, which was his name, "what must I do for it? I am ready!" "Baba Mustapha," said Morgiana, "thou must take thy sewing materials, and come with me, and I will blindfold thee until thou comest to a certain place."

Baba Mustapha hesitated a little at these words, but after some persuasion he went with Morgiana, who, when she had bound his eyes with a handkerchief, led him to her deceased master's house, and never unbandaged his eyes until he had entered the room where she had put the quarters. "Baba Mustapha," said she, "make haste and sew these quarters together, and when thou hast done so, I will give thee another piece of gold."

After Baba Mustapha had finished his task, Morgiana blindfolded him, gave him another piece of gold, and recommending secrecy, led him to his shop, and unbandaged his eyes. She then returned home, and prepared Cassim's body for the funeral, which was held the next day with the usual pomp and ceremony.

Three or four days after the funeral Ali Baba removed his few goods openly to the widow's house, but the money he had taken from the robbers he conveyed thither by night. Soon after his marriage with his sister-in-law was celebrated, and as these marriages were customary in his country, nobody was surprised. As for Cassim's warehouse Ali Baba gave it to his eldest son.

Let us now leave Ali Baba to enjoy the beginning of his fortune, and return to the forty thieves. They came again to their retreat in the forest, but great was their surprise to find Cassim's body taken away, with some of their bags of gold. "We are certainly discovered," said the captain, "and if we do not speedily apply some remedy, shall gradually lose all the riches which our ancestors and ourselves have been many years amassing with so much pain and danger. It is evident that the thief whom we surprised, has an accomplice, and now that one of the villains has been caught we must discover the other. One of you who is bold, artful and enterprising must go into the town, disguised as a traveller. He will thus be able to ascertain whether any man has lately died a strange death. But in case this messenger return to us with a false report, I ask you all, if ye do not think that he should suffer death?" All the robbers found the captain's pro-

posal so advisable that they unanimously approved of it.
Thereupon one of the robbers started up and requested
to be sent into the town. He received great commenda-
tion from the captain and his comrades, disguised himself and taking his leave of the band, went into the town
just before daybreak. He walked up and down until acci-
dentally he came to Baba Mustapha's stall, which was
always open before any of the other shops.

Baba Mustapha was seated with an awl in his hand.
The robber saluted him, and perceiving that he was old,
said: "Honest man, thou beginnest work very early. Is it
possible that one of thine age can see so well?" "Certainly," said Baba Mustapha, "thou must be a stranger,
and do not know me. I have extraordinary eyes, and thou
wilt not doubt it, when I tell thee that I sewed a dead
body together, in a place where I had not so much light as
I have now."

The robber was overjoyed at this information, and pro-
ceeded to question Baba Mustapha until he learned all
that had occurred. He then pulled out a piece of gold and
putting it into the cobbler's hand, said to him: "I can assure thee that I will never divulge thy secret. All that I
ask of thee is to show me the house where thou stitchedst
up the dead body. Come, let me blind thine eyes at the
same place, where the slave girl bound them. We will
walk on together, and perhaps thou mayest go direct to
the house, where occurred thy mysterious adventure. As
everybody ought to be paid for his trouble, here is a
second piece of gold for thee." So saying he put another
piece of gold in Baba Mustapha's hand.

The two pieces of gold were a great temptation to the
cobbler. He looked at them a long time, without saying
a word, thinking what he should do, but at last he pulled

out his purse, and put them into it. He then rose up, to the great joy of the robber, and said: "I do not assure thee that I shall be able to remember the way, but since thou desirest it, I will try what I can do."

The robber, who had his handkerchief ready, tied it over Baba Mustapha's eyes and walked by him until he stopped, partly leading him, and partly guided by him. "I think," said Baba Mustapha, "that I went no farther," and he had now stopped before Cassim's house, where Ali Baba lived. The robber before he pulled off the bandage from the cobbler's eyes, marked the door with a piece of chalk, which he had ready in his hand, and finding that he could discover nothing more from Baba Mustapha, he thanked him for the trouble he had taken, and let him go back to his stall. After this the robber rejoined his band in the forest, and triumphantly related his good fortune.

A little after the robber and Baba Mustapha had departed, Morgiana went out of Ali Baba's house upon an errand, and upon her return, seeing the mark that the robber had made, stopped to observe it. "What can be the meaning of this mark?" said she to herself. "Somebody means my master no good!" Accordingly she fetched a piece of chalk, and marked two or three doors on each side, in the same manner, without saying a word to her master or mistress.

Meanwhile the robber captain had armed his men, and he said to them: "Comrades, we have no time to lose, let us set off well armed, but without its appearing who we are. That it may not excite suspicion, let only one or two go into the town together, and join our rendezvous, which shall be the great square. In the meantime I will go with our comrade, who brought us the good news, and find the house, that we may decide what had best be done."

This speech and plan were approved of by all, and soon they were ready. They filed off in parties of two each, and got into the town without being in the least suspected. The robber who had visited the town in the morning, led the captain into the street where he had marked Ali Baba's residence, and when they came to the first of the houses, which Morgiana had marked, he pointed it out. But the captain observed that the next door was marked in the same manner. The robber was so confounded that he knew not what explanation to make, but was still more puzzled when he saw five or six houses similarly marked.

The captain finding that their expedition had failed, went directly to the place of rendezvous, and told the members of the band that all was lost, and that they must return to their cave. He himself set them the example, and they all returned secretly as they had come. When they were gathered together, the captain told his comrades what had occurred, and the robber spy was declared by all to be worthy of death. The spy condemned himself, acknowledging that he ought to have taken more precaution and he received with courage the stroke from him who was appointed to cut off his head.

But as the safety of the band required that an injury should not go unpunished, another robber offered to go into the town and see what he could discover. His offer being accepted, he went, and finding Baba Mustapha, gave him a gold piece, and, being shown Ali Baba's house, marked it, in an inconspicuous place, with red chalk. Not long after Morgiana, whose eye nothing could escape, went out, and seeing the red chalk, marked the other neighbors' houses in the same place and manner.

The second robber spy, on his return to the cave, reported his adventure, and the captain and all the band were overjoyed at the thought of immediate success. They went into the town, with the same precautions as before, but when the robber and his captain came to the street, they found a number of houses marked alike with red chalk. At this the captain was enraged, and retired with his band to the cave, where the robber spy was condemned to death, and was immediately beheaded.

The captain, having lost two brave fellows of his band, and being afraid lest he should lose more, resolved to take upon himself the important commission. Accordingly he went and addressed himself to Baba Mustapha who did him the same service he had done for the other robbers. The captain did not mark the house with chalk, but examined it so carefully, that it was impossible for him to mistake it. Well satisfied with his attempt, he returned to the forest, and when he came to the cave, where the band awaited him, said: "Now, comrades, nothing can prevent our full revenge, as I am certain of the house." He then ordered the members of the band to go into the villages round about, and buy nineteen mules, and thirty-eight large leathern jars, one full of oil, and the others empty.

In two or three days' time the robbers had purchased the mules and the jars. The captain, after putting one of his men into each jar, rubbed the outside of the vessels with oil. Things being thus prepared, when the nineteen mules were loaded with the thirty-seven robbers in jars, and the jar of oil, the captain, as their driver, set out with them, and reached the town by the dusk of the evening, as he had intended. He led the mules through the streets, until he came to Ali Baba's house, at whose door he stopped. Ali Baba was sitting there after supper to take a little fresh air, and the captain addressed him and said: "I have brought some oil a great distance, to sell at to-morrow's market, and it is now so late that I do not know where to lodge. If I should not be troublesome to thee, do me the favor to let me pass the night in thy house." Though Ali Baba had seen the robber captain in the forest, and had heard him speak, it was impossible to know him in the disguise of an oil merchant. He told him that he should be welcome, and immediately opened his gates for the mules to pass through into the yard. At the same time he called a slave, and ordered him to fodder the mules. He then went to Morgiana, to bid her prepare a good supper for his guest.

Supper was served, after which the robber captain withdrew to the yard, under pretense of looking after his mules. Beginning at the first jar, and so on to the last, he said to each man: "As soon as I throw some stones out of my chamber window, cut the jar open with the knife thou hast for that purpose, and come out, and I will immediately join thee." After this he returned to the house, and Morgiana, taking a light, conducted him to his chamber, where she left him.

Now, Morgiana, returning to her kitchen, found that there was no oil in the house, and, as her lamp went out, she did not know what to do, but presently bethinking herself of the oil jars, she went into the yard. When she came nigh to the first jar, the robber within said softly: "Is it time?" Though the robber spoke low, Morgiana heard him distinctly, for the captain, when he unloaded the mules, had taken the lids off the jars to give air to his men, who were ill at ease, and needed room to breathe.

Morgiana was naturally surprised at finding a man in a jar instead of the oil she wanted, but she immediately comprehended the danger to Ali Baba, and his family, and the necessity of applying a speedy remedy without noise. Collecting herself, without showing the least emotion, she answered: "Not yet, but presently." She went in this manner to all the jars, giving the same answer, until she came to the jar of oil.

By this means, Morgiana found that her master, Ali Baba, who thought that he was entertaining an oil-merchant, had really admitted thirty-eight robbers into his house, including the pretended oil-merchant, who was their captain. She made what haste she could to fill her oil pot, and returned to her kitchen, and, as soon as she lighted her lamp, she took a great kettle, went again to the oil jar, filled the kettle, set it upon a large wood fire, and as soon at it boiled, went, and poured enough into every jar to stifle and destroy the robber within. She then returned to her kitchen, put out the light, and resolved that she would not go to rest, until she had observed what might happen, through a window which opened into the yard.

She had not waited long before the captain of the robbers gave the appointed signal, by throwing little stones, several of which hit the jars. He then listened, and not hearing or perceiving any movement among his companions, became uneasy and descended softly into the yard. Going to the first jar he smelt the boiled oil, which sent forth a steam, and examining the jars one after the other he found all of his band dead, and by the oil that he missed out of the last jar, guessed the means and manner of their death. Hence he suspected that his plot to murder Ali Baba and plunder his house was discovered. Enraged to despair at having failed in his design, he forced the lock of a door that led from the yard to the garden, and climbing over the walls, he made his escape. Morgiana satisfied and pleased to have succeeded so well, in saving her master and his family, went to bed.

The next morning Morgiana took Ali Baba aside and communicated to him the events of the preceding night. Astonished beyond measure Ali Baba examined all the jars, in each of which was a dead robber. He stood for some time motionless, now looking at the jars, and now at Morgiana, without saying a word, so great was his surprise. At last, when he had recovered himself, he said: "I will not die without rewarding thee as thou deservest! I owe my life to thee, and, as the first token of my gratitude, I give thee thy liberty from this moment, and later I will complete thy recompense! I am persuaded with thee that the forty robbers had laid snares for my destruction. Allah by thy means hath delivered me from their wicked designs, and I hope he will continue to do so, and that he will deliver the world from their persecution and from their cursed race. All we now have to do, is to bury the bodies of these pests of mankind."

Ali Baba's garden was very long, and there he and his slaves dug a pit in which they buried the robbers, and levelled the ground again. After which Ali Baba returned to his house and hid the jars and weapons; the mules he sold in the market. While Ali Baba was thus employed, the captain of the forty robbers returned to the forest, and entered the cave. He there sat down to consider how he could revenge himself upon Ali Baba.

The loneliness of the gloomy cavern became frightful

to him. "Where are ye, my brave comrades," cried he,
"old companions of my watchings, and labors? What can
I do without you? Did I collect you only to lose you by so
base a fate, and so unworthy of your courage? Had ye
died with your sabres in your hands, like brave men, my
regret had been less! When shall I enlist so gallant a band
again? I will truly revenge you upon this miserable Ali
Baba, and will provide new masters for all this gold and
treasure, who shall preserve and augment it to all posterity!" This resolution being taken, the captain feeling
more easy in his mind, and full of hopes, slept all night
very quietly.

When he awoke early next morning, he disguised himself as a merchant, and going into the town, took a lodg-
ing at an inn. He gradually conveyed, from the cavern to
the inn, a great many rich stuffs, and fine linens. He then
took a shop opposite to Cassim's warehouse, which Ali
Baba's son had occupied since the death of his uncle.
Within a few days the pretended merchant had culti-
vated a friendship with the son, caressed him in the most
engaging manner, made him small presents, and asked
him to dine and sup with him.

Ali Baba's son did not choose to lie under such obliga-
tions to the pretended merchant, without making the like
return; he therefore acquainted his father with his desire
to return these favors. Ali Baba, with great pleasure,
took the entertainment upon himself, and invited his son
to bring his friend to supper; he then gave orders to Morgiana to prepare a fine repast.

The pretended merchant accompanied the son to Ali
Baba's house, and after the usual salutations, said: "I beg
of thee not to take it amiss that I do not remain for supper, for I eat nothing that has salt in it, therefore judge

how I should feel at thy table!" "If that be all," replied Ali
Baba, "it ought not to deprive me of thy company at supper, for I promise thee that no salt shall be put in any
meat or bread served this night. Therefore thou must do
me the favor to remain."

Ali Baba then went into the kitchen, and commanded
Morgiana to put no salt in the meat that was dressed
that night. Morgiana, who was always ready to obey
her master, was much dissatisfied at this peculiar order.
"Who is this strange man," she asked, "who eats no salt in
his meat? Does he not know that the eating of salt by host
and guest cements forever the bond of friendship?" "Do
not be angry, Morgiana," said Ali Baba, "he is an honest
man, therefore do as I bid."

Morgiana obeyed, though with reluctance, and was
filled with curiosity to see this man who would eat no salt
with his host. To this end she helped Ali Baba to carry up
the dishes, and looking at the pretended merchant, she
knew him at first sight, notwithstanding his disguise, to
be the captain of the forty robbers, and examining him
carefully, she perceived that he had a dagger under his
garment.

Thus having penetrated the wicked design of the pretended merchant, Morgiana left the hall, and retiring to
her own chamber, dressed herself as a dancer, and girded
her waist with a silver girdle, to which there hung a poniard. When she had thus clad herself she said to a slave:
"Take thy tabour, and let us go, and divert our master
and his son's guest." The slave took his tabour, and played
all the way into the hall before Morgiana, who immediately began to dance in such a manner as would have created admiration in any company.

After she had danced several dances with equal grace,

she drew the poniard, and holding it in her hand, began a dance of light movements, and surprising leaps. Sometimes she presented the poniard to one breast, then to another, and oftentimes seemed to strike her own. At length Morgiana presented the poniard to the breast of the pretended merchant, and with a courage worthy of herself, plunged it into his heart.

Ali Baba and his son, shocked at this action, cried out aloud. "Unhappy wretch!" exclaimed Ali Baba, "what hast thou done to ruin me and my family!" "It was to preserve, not to ruin thee," answered Morgiana, opening the pretended merchant's garment, and showing the dagger. "See what an enemy thou hast entertained! Look well at him, and thou wilt find both the false oil-merchant, and the captain of the band of forty robbers. Remember too that he would eat no salt with thee, and wouldest thou have more to persuade thee of his wicked design?"

Ali Baba, overcome with gratitude, embraced Morgiana, and said: "Morgiana, I gave thee thy liberty, and now I will marry thee to my son, who will consider himself fortunate to wed the preserver of his family." Ali Baba then turned and questioned his son, who far from showing any dislike, readily consented to the marriage, not only because he wished to obey his father, but because it was agreeable to his inclinations. A few days after, Ali Baba celebrated the nuptials of his son and Morgiana, with great solemnity, a sumptuous feast, and the usual dancing.

Ali Baba and his son buried the captain of the robbers with his comrades, and at the end of a year, seeing that he had not been molested by any other robbers, Ali Baba mounted his horse and set out for the cave. When he arrived there he pronounced the words, "Open Sesame,"

and the door immediately opened. From the condition of
the treasures he judged that no one had visited the cave
since the band of forty robbers had been destroyed. He
put upon his horse as much gold as he could carry, and
returned home.

Afterwards, Ali Baba took his son to the cave, taught
him its secret, which they handed down to their posterity,
who ever after, using their good fortune with modera-
tion, lived in great honor and splendor.

11

SHEN OF THE SEA

◇◇◇

" 'WE ARE THE SHEN, DEMONS OF THE SEA,'
ANSWERED THE SEVEN. 'WE ARE SHEN OF
THE OCEAN, AND WE COME TO CLAIM OUR
OWN.' "

◇◇◇

Kua Hai City stands on a plain in northern China.
The plain is called Wa Tien, and it is very smooth and
fertile, giving many large melons. . . . Life there is
good. The plain is likewise extremely low. Any reliable
geography will tell you that Kua Hai is below sea level.
And that, I know, is a fact, for I, lazily seated in my garden, have often gazed at sailing ships, large-eyed—wide-
staring-eyed junks as they fetched into the Bay of The
Sharp-Horned Moon, and to view them I had to raise my
eyes. It is very true. I had to look up, as one looks up to
behold the sky-hung eagles of Lo Fan.

I had as often wondered if the sea ever broke through
its restraining walls and flooded Kua Hai. A storm coming down from the northeast would most likely thrust
billows to overtop the wall. So I said to my gardener, Wu

Chang: "Wu Chang, did fishes ever swim up the Street of A Thousand Singing Dragons? Did the sea ever come into Kua Hai?" Wu Chang paused in his scratching among the *hung lo po* (the radishes). Since thinking it over, I am inclined to believe that he welcomed an opportunity to change from the working of his fingers to the working of his tongue. "Once, and once only, Honorable One, has the sea invaded Kua Hai. But it can never do so again. Chieh Chung was fooled once, but he was far too clever to be fooled twice. He buried the bottle, perhaps in this very garden, for who knows? He buried it so deep that no ordinary digging shall discover it. And so, the sea may look over the walls of Kua Hai, but it may not enter."

"Indeed?" said I. "And pray, who *was* this Chieh Chung? And what was in the bottle?"

Such astounding ignorance gained me a look of compassion from old Wu Chang. "The Honorable One is surely jesting. He, of course, knows that Chieh Chung was the first King of Wa Tien."

"Oh, to be sure," I interrupted. "It was Chieh Chung who invented—hum—er radishes." That was a guess, and a miss.

Wu Chang corrected me. "Not radishes, but writing. A mistaken thing to do, in my opinion. But beyond doubt he did a great service when he bottled the water demons. Ho. Ho. Ho. He bottled the demons as if they were melon pickles. Ho. Ho. Ho."

"Sit here in the shade, Wu Chang," said I. "So Chieh Chung pickled the water demons—and then what?"

"Not pickled, Honorable One, bottled. Chieh Chung bottled the demons. Ho. Ho. Ho. . . . You must understand that in those days the plain hereabouts was much lower than it is now. It had not been built up. And the

sea was much higher in those days, for then there were
no heavy ships to weigh it down, and flatten it. The sea
was very high then-a-days, far too high for its breadth.
On every side the land held it back, and it was retarded
and had no freedom of motion. So the Shen, the demons
of the sea, got them together and took thought. They
said: 'Our sea is far too small. We must have more room.
We are mighty, are we not? Then let us take some land
and occupy it, so that our sea may expand.'

"Accordingly, the water demons swam along the coast,
seeking land to conquer. They passed the shores of Fu
Sang without stopping, for that region is high and moun-
tainous. They passed the region of San Shen Shan, for in
that place lives the powerful land demon named Hu
Kung. The water demons were in no great haste to gain
Hu Kung's hatred. They passed without a second glance.
But when the Shen swam up to Kua Hai, it was to rejoice.
The demons looked over the wall; they smiled down

upon Kua Hai and said, 'This land we shall take for our
beloved sea. It is low, and suited to our purpose. Right-
fully it is ours. Yes, we shall take Kua Hai, and all the vast
plain hereabout.' But the ocean demons were possessed
of decency. They did not dash over the walls, calling on
their sea to follow, and so drown all the people of Kua
Hai. Demons though they be, the Shen that time had
mercy in their hearts. While the night dew lay upon the
fields of Wa Tien, those demons, to the number of seven,
made their way into Kua Hai. There they waited in the
garden of the palace.

"When King Chieh Chung, who ruled over Wa Tien,
took him to the garden for an early morning stroll, he discovered the demons waiting. He knew at once they were
no ordinary men. Not once did they *kou tou* (knock their
heads on the ground) as men should do. Nor did they look
like the men of Wa Tien. Their mouths were wide mouths,
like those of codfishes. Their bodies were covered with
iridescent scales. Nevertheless, Chieh Chung permitted
the Shen to approach. 'What manner of men are you?'
asked the King. 'And what is your pleasure?'

" 'We are the Shen, demons of the sea,' answered the seven. 'We are Shen of the ocean, and we come to claim our own.' 'And what is that?' asked the King, smiling tolerantly upon them, though in truth he felt more like weeping, for he knew what would be the answer.

" 'We have come to possess ourselves of the city and all the low plain that surrounds it. It is our right, and our might—we mean to have it.' Then Chieh Chung's heart dropped down to a level with his sandals. His heart was weighted as if with millstones, as if weighted with Mount Tai. Long he stroked his beard, pondering, grieving, praying. And the water demons danced in the dew. Jubilant were they, flinging their toes high, spattering dewdrops upon the palace roof, and singing the terrible song of the ocean.

"Finally the King answered. 'Shen,' said he, 'what time do you grant me? Kua Hai is a large city. In it are half a million souls. It will be moons and moons before I can count my people safely upon the Mountain of The Yellow Ox.' One of the demons was shaking a *pai shu* (shaking a cypress tree) so that its dew fell upon him and upon his companions, for already the sun was up and they were beginning to feel the day and its dryness. 'What time?' said the Shen, taking his answer from the *pai shu*. 'We shall give you until this tree is in flower. Have all your people gathered upon high ground when this *pai shu* blossoms, for at that time we shall lead the sea upon Wa Tien, and the sea shall stand three *li* deep above your palace. That is our answer. And now we must go for the sun has lit his fire.'

"The Shen made a move as if to depart, but no sooner were they out of the shadows than they halted abruptly, murmuring in displeasure. And small wonder. The sun

had dispelled the dew and there was no moisture upon
the land. A water Shen cannot exist where there is no
moisture. In that respect he is like the *yin yu* and the *shih
pan* (fishes). So the Shen turned to Chieh Chung and
said, 'Is there water here, O King, where we may spend
the day hours?' 'There is little,' said Chieh Chung; 'I dare
say too little for your purpose. But in such quantity as it
is, you are welcome.' He pointed to a crystal bowl in
which burgeoned a sacred lily. There was water in the
bowl, water surrounding the lily bulb. Too, there were
stones in the bowl—blue lapis lazuli, and green jade,
and yellow topaz (precious stones, as befitted a palace
garden), for that is the way sacred lilies are grown—in
bowls filled with water and pretty pebbles. 'You are quite
welcome to it,' reiterated the King. The Shen shook their
heads half in despair. 'It is too little,' groaned they,
'far too little.' 'But,' said Chieh Chung, 'you are demons
—hence magicians. Why do you not make yourselves
smaller? Why not change yourselves into red *hung pao
shih* and recline in the bowl amid the lily roots? I am sure
you would make handsome rubies. Beyond a doubt, my
courtiers would say "Ah" and "How lovely" and admire
you greatly when they saw you. Of a certainty, you would
make resplendent gems, dazzling and superb.' 'Well,'
agreed the Shen, somewhat dubiously, 'we shall try it. If
you have no more water it is the only thing we *can* do.'
And so, in a twinkling the Shen were gone, and seven
beautiful rubies appeared in the crystal bowl.

"'How lovely,' said Chieh Chung—and deliberately
winked at the cypress tree, first with one eye and then
with the other. He went to a cabinet that stood in his
chamber, and from the cabinet took a bottle fashioned
out of *fei yu* (a cloudy jade). And the bottle had a wide

mouth. Into it Chieh Chung poured water. Returning to
the lily bowl, he quickly took therefrom the seven red
hung pao shih and dropped them into the jade bottle—
closing the mouth securely.

" 'Now,' exulted the King, 'my city is saved. My people
may walk in security and without fear. The seven water
demons are in my keeping, and please Heaven may they
never escape my hand.' And in his joy, King Chieh Chung
ordered that ten thousand catties of rice be given to the
poor.

"Weeks lengthened into months. Lengthened the
months to years. Still languished the water demons in the
clouded jade bottle. Still broke the sea on Kua Hai's walls
—but did not enter. Chieh Chung added to his kingdom and ruled with beneficence. His name was heralded
throughout the length of the world. Not by the spear, but
by wisdom he added to his dominions. Peoples of far-
distant regions came seeking to place themselves under
the rule of Chieh Chung—wisest and best.

"At length came ambassadors from Wei Chou, yes,
even from distant Kou Pei, offering to give their al-
legiance to Chieh Chung. Ah, but that was a great day,
a day of all proud days. The ambassadors were a hundred
for number, haughty mandarins all. There was a great stir
about the palace, you may well believe, retainers rushing
hither and thither to provide food and drink and entertainment for the foreign great men.

"A foolish servant, ransacking cupboard and closet for
what victuals and drink he could find, came upon the
dusty jade bottle that stood in Chieh Chung's cabinet.
'Ah,' said the servant, trying to peer through the cloudy
jade. 'Beyond a doubt, here is something of rare ex-

cellence. This will do for the highest of the mandarins, for the red-button mandarins with peacock feathers. It rattles—rock candy in it.' And the foolish one removed the stopper. A thousand pities he was not stricken dead before the seal was broken.

"Chieh Chung came into the chamber and saw what had happened. For a moment he was stunned. Then, 'Let me have the bottle.' The bottle was empty, all save for a bit of water. 'They are gone,' said the King. 'The Shen have escaped. But even so, I may baffle them, for they promised with binding oaths not to take my kingdom until the *pai shu* blossoms. And—in this region the cypress tree never blossoms—it *never* comes into flower.' The King smiled in spite of himself.

"Meanwhile, the water demons, having escaped from the bottle, hastened through the palace toward the garden. They were very angry—were those demons, gnashing their teeth with a noise like that of waves lashing a rock-guarded coast. They were determined on vengeance.

"The Wei Chou ambassadors were encamped in the palace garden. Their servants had been washing garments, brilliant-hued garments such as the wealthy and noble of that land wear. The garments had been hung on the cypress tree to dry. And there the garments hung when the water demons appeared. The tree was aflame with color. Instantly the Shen raised a great shout. 'Come billow. Come ocean.' They shouted in triumph. 'The *pai shu* blossoms (the cypress tree blooms)'—for they thought the garments were flowers—'and our promise is ended. Kua Hai is ours.'

"Fathoms deep, roaring, grinding, relentless, the sea

swept over Kua Hai, buried the city, buried the plain.
The water demons raced before it, calling it on. They
who had been the people of Kua Hai rode upon white-
crested billows—without life—drowned. Out of all the
vast population perhaps a thousand escaped. And among
those who escaped was the King.

"Chieh Chung sat under a pine tree on the mountain,
grief-stricken, heartbroken, gazing upon what had been
a city, and now was sparkling sea. Hour after hour sat the
King, grieving and thinking, meditating a way to regain
his country. Now and then the seven water demons appeared before him, mocking, splashing him with spray.

"One day, having meditated long, Chieh Chung arose
and shouted exultantly: 'I have it. I know how I shall regain my city. I shall go immediately and put the plan in
writing, while it is fresh in my mind.' Having said, he
walked to the little hut that served for his palace and sat
down at a table to write. On the table stood a crystal
bowl, with a lily, and with green, blue, and yellow stones.

"Chieh Chung sat writing meaningless stuff upon
parchment. All the while he kept an eye on the crystal
bowl. Lo. There appeared seven red stones at the root of
the lily. The demons had come to spy upon the King's
writing. They had come to learn his plan, and so triumph
over him. But they, unwittingly, were giving themselves
into bondage again. For Chieh Chung quickly thrust
them into a bottle and sealed it against all escape. Six of
the demons he thus imprisoned. The seventh, who was a
small fellow, Chieh Chung threw back into the sea. 'Go,'
said the King, 'and take your sea with you. Take your sea,
and never trouble me again. Else I shall most certainly
destroy your six brothers. It is a warning.'

"So the seventh demon sped away, taking the sea with

him. Then did Chieh Chung descend to Kua Hai and build up the city, people coming in from far countries. Once more the city was inhabited, and the land was more rich, by reason of its flooding.

"And the six Shen, the six water demons are buried deep, in a jade bottle—perhaps under this very garden."

12

THE BOY WHO STOLE THE NIGHTINGALE THAT WAS CALLED GIZARI

◆◇◇◇◇◇◇◇◇◇◇◇◇◇◇◇◇◇◇◇◇◇◇◇◇◇◇◇◇◇◇◇◇◇◇◇◇◇◇◆

"IT LACKS ONE SINGLE THING, WITHOUT WHICH IT CANNOT BE PERFECT. IT IS THE NIGHT-INGALE CALLED GIZARI. IF THOU HADST HER TO SING IN IT, THERE WOULD INDEED BE NONE OTHER SUCH A MOSQUE IN THE WHITE WORLD."

◇◇◇◇◇◇◇◇◇◇◇◇◇◇◇◇◇◇◇◇◇◇◇◇◇◇◇◇◇◇◇◇◇◇◇◇◇◇◆

O nce—however it came about, let it be as it may!—there was a King of this Land-of-the-Eagles who died, leaving three sons to rule the kingdom together after him. The first was named Imer, the second was named Marash, and the third was named Rasím.

After they had buried him and mourned for him properly Imer, the eldest, said to the others, "Our father was a great king and built many palaces and mosques for the worship of God. We should walk in his footsteps. I, being the eldest son, shall build a mosque more splendid than the largest of his, in which only I may kneel to pray, so that all men shall know my nobleness."

Accordingly he took a half of all the gold his father had left to him as his share, and summoned the greatest architects and built a mosque of tile, with a minaret taller than any in the capital, and spread on its floor a costly silken carpet, and over its door he placed a golden tablet on which was engraved, "None may pray here but I, Imer the Great."

Now the fame of the mosque and its richness went abroad, and each day, as he knelt alone on its splendid carpet, Imer grew more prideful. But the kings of neighboring countries, who journeyed there to see it, when they read the tablet over its door, went away smiling.

One day when he went there he saw standing before it an aged Dervish with a long white beard and a green turban. Said he to the stranger, "What thinkest thou of this mosque which I have built? Surely there can be none to compare with it in the white world."

The Dervish, however, combing his long beard with his fingers, made no reply, so that Imer said, "It is difficult, no doubt, for thee to find words to express thy admiration. Nevertheless, do thy best and it will not displease me." But still the Dervish remained silent.

Then Imer was filled with anger, and cried he, "Say in one word whether this mosque is not the most glorious of all in any land beneath the sun!"

Said the Dervish then, "It lacks one thing, without which it will never be perfect." And with the words he departed.

Imer went to the palace in an ill-humor, saying to himself, "The Dervish is a donkey!" But remembering how the kings who had seen the mosque had gone away smiling, he thought, "Perhaps, indeed, it does lack something of perfection, which they noticed." And day by day his dissatisfaction grew, till at last he pulled it down to its foundation stones and threw the tiles of which it had been built into the river.

When his brothers saw the mosque in ruins, they asked him, "Why hast thou done this?" He replied, "It lacked something, though I know not what."

Then Marash, the second of the three, said, "In my turn I shall build a mosque." And he spent three quarters of the gold his father had left him for materials and built one of gray stone that was even larger and handsomer than Imer's had been. It had carved doorways and crimson curtains, and over its entrance was inscribed, "Only Beys of noble birth may pray in this mosque of Marash." So splendid was it that nobles of the whole countryside came to kneel in it. The common people, however, when they learned the meaning of the characters written over its entrance, made a mock of it and threw fish-heads in the street before it. But Marash took great pride in it and said a prayer in it every day.

One afternoon, as he was about to enter its door, he saw on the threshold the white-bearded Dervish with the green turban. Said he, "Men call this mosque of mine the finest in any land. Thinkest thou not they speak truly?"

The Dervish, however, cast his eyes upward and said nothing. Then Marash said to him, "Canst thou not speak? Is there any more splendid on the earth?" But to this also the stranger was silent. So that Marash, angered, exclaimed, "Thou tongueless dolt! Answer me, or it will go hard with thee!"

Then the Dervish said, "One thing thy mosque lacks, without which it can never be perfect." And with the words he mingled with the crowd of the street.

Marash went to the palace in rage, thinking, "What does the ignorant lout know of real splendor?" But as he thought, he remembered the fish-heads, and said to himself, "Can it be that the Dervish is right, and that there is in fact something missing in the structure that even common people have perceived?" The more he reflected, the more dissatisfied he grew, till in the end he had the building pulled down, so that not one stone was left upon another.

When his brothers Imer and Rasím saw what he had done, they questioned him and he replied that, beautiful as it was, it missed the perfection he had desired and no longer pleased him.

Then said Rasím, the youngest, "It is my turn now to build one." And he took all the fortune his father had left to him and bought white marble, and built of it a mosque neither large nor small, but as lovely as a white flower, over whose entrance was engraved these words: "Let all who will enter freely to pray with Rasím."

Now though the building was not of great size, it was so beautiful that folk talked of it more than they had talked of both the others put together, and there was no day when visitors from afar did not come to see it. The inscription over its doorway pleased noble and humble, rich and poor, and all who prayed in it praised its builder's wisdom and modesty.

One evening, as Rasím rose from his prayer, he saw standing in its doorway the old Dervish of the white beard and green turban, and he said to him, "I am the builder of this mosque and I desire it to be a thing unsurpassed. Has it, in thine eyes, any lack which I may make good?"

Twice he repeated the words and the Dervish made no reply. The third time, however, he answered, "It lacks one single thing, without which it cannot be perfect."

Said Rasím, then, "Glory to thy tongue! I pray thee tell me what it is, that I may supply it."

The Dervish answered, "It is the nightingale called Gizari. If thou hadst her to sing in it, there would indeed be none other such a mosque in the white world."

Asked Rasím, "Where is that nightingale to be found?"

The Dervish replied, "That I cannot tell thee. I only know that its song is the most beautiful that man's ear has ever heard."

Rasím went to his brothers Imer and Marash and told them what the Dervish had said. Exclaimed Imer, "Insolent rascal! Why did he not tell me?" And cried Marash, "He might have told me as well! If he shows his face again he shall lose his ears!" But Rasím said, "Let us start out together in search of the nightingale Gizari, and if we find her, when she is singing in the mosque we shall know that by our mutual efforts it has reached perfection and God will favor us equally. And, since we are the sons of a King and it does not become us to fail, let us swear that we will not return without her."

The other two agreed to this and they bade their ministers rule wisely during their absence, and set out on the road, asking every traveler they met if he knew where the bird was to be found. But each of them answered, "Though we have listened to many tales of this and that, of the nightingale called Gizari we have never heard."

Now when they had journeyed thus for twenty days
they came one morning to a place where stood a white
stone, where the road forked into three trails, and Rasím
said, "Let us separate here and each take a different trail.
And let the one who finds the nightingale return here
and go in search of the others."

This seemed good to the rest and they kissed one another, saying, "Mayest thou go on a smooth road!" and
set out, each in a different direction.

The trail which Imer, the eldest, took led to the north,
and he went as far as he went till he grew tired. Said he
to himself, "Of what use is it to plod forever up one side
of a mountain and down the other, searching for what
may not be anywhere? For how do we know but that the
Dervish lied? I will wager he never heard of a nightingale
called Gizari!" But he dreaded to return to his home lest
he be shamed by the breaking of his oath, and coming to
a pleasant town nestled in a fruitful valley, he appren-
ticed himself to a barber, and made his living by shaving
men's heads.

Marash's trail pointed southward, and he went as far
as he went till he also became weary of the journeying.
Said he to himself, "One may trudge this trail to the very
end of the earth without finding the cursèd bird!" And
he, too, remembered the oath he had sworn and dreaded
to return, and coming to a prosperous city on the bank
of a river, he opened a coffee stall in its bazaar and made
his livelihood by selling coffee to the merchants and
tradesmen.

So Imer and Marash, having no heart for the toil of the
way, gave over the search and each looked after his own
affairs. As for Rasím, the youngest, however, he followed
his trail, which led to the eastward, for three months,

till he came to a land that was wild and desolate, in the midst of savage mountains, where was neither farm nor roadhouse nor dwelling, but only rough rocks and fir trees.

As he threaded these wastes he came one morning to a woman, clad only in a robe of twisted tree bark, who was combing her tangled hair with a stick. Pitying her condition, he took his comb from his girdle bag and combed her hair for her, cleaning it of the dust and leaves it had gathered, at which she was greatly pleased. Said she, "O Stranger, never have I seen a thing like that. What is its name?"

"It is called a comb," he answered. "If thou wilt I will give it to thee."

She said, "Folk do not give for nothing, and what have I to offer thee in exchange?"

He replied, "Thou hast only to answer a question."

She asked, "What is thy question?" and he said, "I am in search of the nightingale called Gizari. In thy wanderings among these mountains hast thou ever heard of her?"

"Never," she answered. "Thou wilt not find her in these parts, where is nothing but rocks and trees. Go back the way thou camest, for beyond here the land is ruled by wild beasts. Even I dare not go there."

"Nevertheless," said he, "I must follow my search."

Then said she, "In return for thy comb, I will tell thee one thing. The next mountain is ruled by a Leopard as huge as an ox. Thou canst pass his domain only by gaining favor of his wife. Thou must speak with her, however, before noon, at which time he returns to his house. If he is there when thou reachest it he will devour thee in three mouthfuls."

Said he, "I shall live or die as God pleases." And bidding her farewell, he went on to the mountain.

It still lacked an hour to noon when he smelled the leopard smell and soon after he came to the Leopard's house, which was built of rocks. Smoke was pouring from its chimney, and looking through its window he saw the Leopard's wife making bread. He knocked at the door and when she opened it she saw him with astonishment.

"What!" she exclaimed. "Art thou a man?"

He replied, "Yes."

Said she, "I have not seen a man since twenty years ago when the Leopard stole me away and brought me here to be his wife. Hasten back the way thou camest, for when he comes he will devour thee!"

Said Rasím, "Let him do what he will with me." And he sat down and watched her make the bread. When she had kneaded the dough and shaped it into loaves, ready to be baked, she opened the door of the stove to sweep the ashes from the hot coals, and he saw that she was sweeping them with her breasts. He bade her wait, and going outside the house, cut some twigs and bound them with his girdle into a broom and with this he swept the fire for her. She was delighted at this. Said she, "Whenever I bake bread for the Leopard I burn my breasts and am abed for ten days afterward! Now I need do so no more."

When the bread was done she broke a loaf and gave him some, and while he was eating it there sounded a dreadful scream from the mountainside. "That is my husband returning!" she exclaimed, and opening the door of the cupboard, she bade him hide in it.

Scarce had he concealed himself when in came the

Leopard, with his claws stretching and his neck hairs bristling—so huge that his shoulders brushed the top of the doorway. Growled he, angrily, "Wife, why hast thou not baked my bread?"

She replied, "I have baked it."

Said he, "How, then, do I find thee on thy feet? Always after the bread-baking thou art ill and unable to rise from thy bed."

She answered, "I have found a way to do it without burning myself." And she set a loaf before him, which he ate, saying, "It is better than the last batch and does not taste of ashes."

Then she asked him, "If I should tell thee that a man had shown me how to bake it thus, wouldst thou eat him?"

"No," he replied. "I would kiss him on the forehead and make him my brother."

When she heard this, she brought Rasím from the cupboard. "Here is the one who showed me," she told him. And the Leopard kissed him on the forehead and asked he, "O my brother, what has brought thee here?"

Said Rasím, "I have built a mosque to the glory of God, but it lacks one thing to make it perfect, and that is the nightingale that is called Gizari. I have searched over a hundred mountains and valleys and still have not found her."

The Leopard answered, "I have heard of her, though I cannot tell thee where she is. My father, the Lion, who rules the next mountain to this, may know, but if he sees thee he will devour thee in two mouthfuls. The only way thou canst find out is through his wife."

"How may I gain favor with her?" asked Rasím.

Said the Leopard, "Thou canst see her only at midafternoon, while the Lion is asleep, when she sits on the doorstep sunning herself. She is a hundred years old and her eyelids cover her eyes like a hat so that she cannot see, but her ears are so keen that she can hear the twitch of a mouse's whisker. So speak to her while thou art still some distance away, before she hears thy step and wakes the Lion to rend thee. Say to her, 'The brother of thy husband's son, the Leopard, greets thee,' and she will receive thee in kindness."

Rasím thanked the Leopard and bade them farewell and went on his way to the next mountain. He walked one hour, he walked two hours, and at length he smelled the lion smell and presently came in sight of the Lion's house, where the Lion's wife sat on the doorstep dozing in the sun. Mindful of the Leopard's warning he stepped as softly as he could, but while he was still a long way off a twig broke under his foot, and she lifted her head. At that he spoke, saying, "O Mother, the brother of thy husband's son, the Leopard, greets thee."

Said she, "Come close and let me see thee."

So he came to her and lifted her eyelids so that she could see him, when she exclaimed, "There is truth in thy face! But thou art a man. What dost thou here, where I have seen no man these many years, since the Lion stole me from my home to be his wife?"

He told her of his search, and she said, "My husband, in truth, knows the nightingale's whereabouts, but the only way I can find out his secrets is by leading him to talk in his sleep."

Just then the Lion, hearing their voices through his slumber, rumbled, "Wife! What sound do I hear?"

She replied, "My dear husband, it is only the wind blowing through the trees."

Said he, "To-morrow I will cut them down!" and turning over, began to snore like twenty wild boars.

Presently she said to Rasím, "Whistle." He did so, and the Lion, hearing in his dream, grunted, "Wife, I hear a sound like a bird singing."

She answered, "Dear husband, it comes over the tree tops. Can it be the song of the nightingale Gizari?"

"Nay," he said, "the land of Queen Bôr, where she is, is too far away for us to hear her."

"It is, then, a cricket chirping," said she, and again he turned over and went to sleep, snarking and snoring like the *bumbullím* of summer thunder.

Then said she to Rasím, "The land of Queen Bôr is to

the eastward, on the other side of the Valley-of-Eagles.
But it is perilous to cross, for the eagles that rule it are
exceedingly fierce, with beaks and claws of iron that will

tear thee in pieces. Thou canst cross it only by night,
when they cannot see thee."

"While I have my sword," Rasím answered, "they shall
not bar me!" And he thanked her and went his way to the
valley below. He reached its edge at sunset, and being
weary, wrapped himself in his cloak and lay down to
sleep beneath a tree. He was awakened at dawn by a
chirping above his head, and looking up saw a snake
coiled in the tree, about to seize three young eaglets in

their nest. He took his girdle knife between his teeth and climbing the tree, killed the snake and threw its body to the ground. Scarce had he descended when a great gray eagle came flying, and alighting beside him, threw off its eagle feathers and became transformed into a woman dressed in a gray robe with a feather headdress.

Said she, "Sir, I thank thee. But for thy blade yonder loathsome serpent would have devoured my fledglings. But what dost thou here, where a man may not come?"

He replied, "I journey to the land of Queen Bôr."

"Thou art on the right trail," said she, "but it is seven days' travel from here, and to reach it thou wilt need the aid of my three sisters. Go straight forward and thou wilt find their house, thatched with eagle feathers, in the center of the valley." Then she took a feather from her headdress and gave it to him. "Show them this and they will aid thee," she said; "but guard thyself well meanwhile."

He thanked her and putting the feather in his girdle, went on across the valley. One day he went, two days he went, and on the third day, as he sat by a stream resting, three fierce eagles darted upon him, screaming and tearing at him with iron beaks and claws. But he drew his sword and fought so strongly that the sharp blade wounded all three, one in the leg, one in the wing, and one in the breast, so that they lay bleeding and helpless.

He sheathed his sword and went on, but before he had gone far pity seized him, and he went back and brought water from the stream, and stripping off his shirt of fine linen, tore it into three pieces and washed and bound up their wounds before he went on.

Whether he went a short way or a long way, he came at length to the house thatched with eagle feathers. The door stood wide and when no one answered his knock he entered and found therein three beds, each with a coverlet of eagles' down, and a table set with three plates, knives, and spoons and a pitcher of water. While he looked about him, he heard the rustling of wings and three gray eagles flew down before the door and throwing off their eagle feathers became transformed into women, wearing gray robes and feather headdresses, and each bore a bandage of white linen, one on her leg, one on her arm, and one on her breast.

They entered, and seeing him, turned pale. But he said to them, "Have no fear," and showing them the feather from his girdle, said, "By this sign I claim your aid." Said they, "It is our sister's. Forgive us that we assailed thee, not knowing thee for her friend." And taking up the pitcher from the table each in turn poured water upon her wound and when they stripped off their bandages the flesh showed no sign of hurt. He related to them how he had saved the three eaglets from the snake, and they exclaimed, "They are our three dear little nephews, and we are beholden to thee. How may we aid thee?"

He replied, "I journey to the land of Queen Bôr."

Said they, "Her capital is three days' travel from here. Stay here with us till to-morrow and we will guide thee and give thee protection on thy trail."

He stayed gladly with them that night, and next morning they donned their eagle feathers and he set out, they flying before him by day and by night circling above him while he slept, till he came within sight of the capital of Queen Bôr. There they flew down and gave him each a feather, saying, "Shouldst thou need our further aid, come to this spot and burn these and we will hasten to thee."

So saying they winged away and he entered the capital, finding it a noble city of towers and gardens. In its center was the Queen's palace and he chose an inn which overlooked its garden and rested there from his long journey.

That evening at dusk as he sat in the inn, he heard a sound so beautiful that he was ravished by it, and said he to the landlord, "What is that?" The man answered, "That is our young Queen's nightingale singing. Each day at this hour she walks with her maidens in the palace garden, where the cage of the nightingale is hung in its pavilion."

Now about the garden was a high wall and when the dark deepened Rasím went there, and tying a stone in the end of his girdle, threw it over the wall and climbed to its top, and thus he beheld the young Queen Bôr—who was so named from her snow-white complexion, the word Bôr meaning snow in that land—strolling among the fruit trees. She was so beautiful that he held his breath to see her, and at first sight he felt his heart fly out of his breast for love of her. Said he to himself, "How can I think to rob her I love of her nightingale? Yet I am bound by mine oath to do so!"

The next day, at twilight, he climbed the wall and presently Queen Bôr came with her maidens from the palace and hanging the nightingale's cage in the pavilion, sat down on the grass beneath a pomegranate tree, while the rest wandered about, plucking and eating the luscious fruits. After a time he heard one say, "The Queen sleeps. Let us go further away so that we shall not waken her with our chatter." And they went into the depths of the garden.

Then Rasím, making no noise, leaped down from the

wall, and stealing to the pavilion, stretched forth his hand
to the cage, and when he touched it the nightingale burst
into sweeter song than ever. But he saw the Queen lying
asleep so near, and her beauty drew him like a rope, so
that he turned from the cage, and bent over her and
kissed her cheek. Instantly, however, she stirred, and
seeing that she was about to waken he made haste to
climb the wall and leap down on the other side.

Waking, Queen Bôr called her maidens, and said to
them, "Go and look in the pavilion and see if my nightingale Gizari is safe." They hastened to look, and returning,
told her, "She sits on her perch, eating caraway seed."
Said the Queen, "I dreamed a man came to steal her
away."

She rose then, and taking the cage from the pavilion,
carried it into the palace, thinking, "The dream has frightened me, for my heart beats strangely." As for Rasím he
went back to the inn angered at himself for having failed
in his purpose.

The next evening he again climbed the wall, and again
the Queen came from the palace with her maidens, and
hanging the cage of the nightingale in the pavilion, said
to them, "Let us play at ball." This they did till she said,
"I am tired and will rest awhile," and they wandered to
the further depths of the garden while she lay down on
the grass and fell asleep. And again Rasím, watching,
leaped down from the wall and crept to the pavilion to
steal the nightingale. But a second time, when he passed
the Queen and saw her loveliness as she slept, her beauty
overcame him and he leaned and kissed her on the
mouth. But at that she stirred, and seeing that she was
about to wake, he ran to the wall and escaped as on the
night before.

Waking, the Queen called her maidens and bade them look in the pavilion and see if the nightingale was safe. Again they returned and told her, "She bathes in her golden bowl." And again she said, "I dreamed a man came to steal her away." And she carried the cage into the palace, saying to herself, "There was more to my dream, that has gone from me, but it has made my heart beat even more strangely than it did yesterday."

Rasím went back to his inn more angered at himself that he had failed a second time in his purpose, and thinking, "With the Queen in my sight I shall never be able to steal the nightingale from her, no, never!" And he lay all that night hopeless and grieving.

The next day, however, he remembered the eagles. He went outside the city to the place where the three eagles had parted from him, and striking fire from his flint and steel, burned the three feathers they had given him.

He waited an hour, he waited two hours, and three hours, and at dusk the eagles flew down from the sky to him and threw off their eagle feathers. Said they, "O our friend! Long life to thee! What is thy need?"

He answered, "Glory to your wings! I came hither to steal from Queen Bôr her nightingale that is called Gizari, but alas! I have fallen deeper than the deep sea in love with her, and my heart fails me!"

Said they, "It will be easy for us to do it for thee, since it sings each evening in the pavilion of the royal garden." And they bade him not to reënter the city, but to make his way to their house in the Valley-of-Eagles. So saying, they donned their feathers and springing into the air, winged swiftly to the city. There they hovered high over the garden of the palace till the Queen had fallen asleep and her maidens wandered away, when they swooped down, and snatching the cage from the pavilion, sped away with it in their talons through the upper air to the house that was thatched with eagle feathers. There at length Rasím arrived, and the nightingale, when she saw him, burst into such song that all the buds on the bushes opened.

Next day the eagles flew with him to the edge of the valley, where they bade him farewell, and he took the backward trail over the mountains, carrying the cage, with the nightingale singing all the way.

He passed the spot where he had killed the snake, and the gray eagle flew down from her nest and threw off her eagle feathers to greet him. He told her of his meeting with her sisters and the aid they had given him, and she said, "Well I knew thou wouldst not fail. Good luck and long life to thee!"

He came at mid-afternoon to the mountain of the Lion, whose wife he found sitting on the doorstep sunning herself. While still a long way off he covered the nightingale's cage with his cloak so that it should not sing, and greeted her as before. And said she, when he had lifted her eyelids so that she could see his face, "Well I knew thou wouldst succeed! A smooth trail to thee!"

Now as before the Lion heard their voices in his sleep, and rumbled, "O Wife! What is the sound I hear?" She answered, "My dear husband, what if it were a man for thee to eat?" Said he, "Cease thy jesting with me when I am sleeping!" And he turned over and began to snore like an avalanche.

Rasím went on to the next mountain, where the Leopard and his wife greeted him in friendship. Said the Leopard, "Well I knew thou wouldst gain the nightingale, O my brother!" And both wished him a fair journey.

Lastly he came to the barren waste of rocks and trees, where he found the wild woman, in her robe of twisted bark, combing her hair with the comb he had given her. Said she, "So thou hast found the nightingale! What wilt thou do with her?"

He replied, "I shall hang her in my mosque and she shall sing while I say my prayers."

Said she, "Well, good luck and long life to thee! Say a prayer for me that I may not break my comb."

Now whether he journeyed a short while or a long while, Rasím came at last to the place of the white stone, where the road forked and where he had parted from his two brothers, and according to their agreement, he set out to find them.

First, he took the northern trail that Imer, his eldest brother, had followed, making inquiry of all he met. So at length he came to the town in which Imer had settled, and seeing a barber's shop, thought, "I will have my head shaved." He hung the cage of the nightingale covered by his cloak in its doorway and entered, and lo, the barber was his brother.

They embraced and kissed one another and when he had exhibited the nightingale, Rasím said, "Do thou dispose of thy business and when we have found our brother Marash, let us go back to our own land and to our proper place."

That same day, therefore, Imer sold his shop and both returned together to the place of the white stone, and set out on the trail to the southward, inquiring of all they met. In time they came to the city on the river bank where Marash had settled. They searched it one day, they searched it two days, and on the third day they sat down before a coffee stall, and lo, the man who served them was the one they sought.

All three embraced and kissed each other, and Rasím said to Marash, "Do thou get rid of thy business, for now we can all return with good hearts to our home." This was done, and next day they started back to their capital.

Now Imer and Marash were ashamed that Rasím had found them in such low employment. When they thought of the fame he would gain for finding the nightingale they were envious and before they had gone ten leagues they hated him. Said Imer secretly to Marash, "Who is he that he should be counted above us?" And Marash answered, "We are the two eldest. Let us so arrange that he shall not trouble us."

So they formed a plan, and when they came to the border of their land they fell upon Rasím and bound and gagged him, smearing his face with clay so that none should know him. When they reached the capital they had him thrown into a windowless dungeon, over which they set a guard of soldiers, giving out that he was a robber, who had attacked them on the road. To their ministers they said, "After terrible hardships and many perils we two have brought the nightingale Gizari. Our brother Rasím, however, while we were in a distant country, was drowned in a mountain stream." So they sat on their thrones again and ruled, and they hung the cage of the nightingale in the mosque of white marble, and folk came from the most distant countries to hear her, and carried the fame of the mosque over the white world.

Thus it was with them. But as for Queen Bôr, when she woke and found that the nightingale had vanished from the pavilion, she was dismayed. She summoned her guard, who searched every bush of the garden, and when the bird could not be found, she sent criers throughout her whole realm, offering a great reward. At last she despatched messengers to many neighboring countries, bidding them bring her word of any bird which might be her lost treasure.

At the end of a year one of these returned and said, "O Queen's Majesty! In the furthest land to which I journeyed, I heard tell of a singing bird in a land still more distant, which is kept in the chief mosque of its capital. While I could not learn by what name it is called, it was said that folk came from near and far to hear it, and by reason of its song the mosque was counted the most famous in the white world."

Exclaimed she, "That is my nightingale!" and she bade him raise a great army, and armed and provisioned it, and putting herself at its head, marched to attack the land of the two Princes, sending heralds in advance to summon them to prepare for the battle.

Now when Imer and Marash learned that a great host was advancing to lay waste their land and capital, they summoned their ministers and asked them, "Why should this be?" The Prime Minister answered, "It has reached us that the Queen who leads the host lays claim to the nightingale Gizari, whose song has made the city's mosque of marble the most famous in the white world."

At this the pair were in great fear. Said they to one another, "Our troops cannot withstand the army that is coming. Let us hide away the nightingale and put a common bird in her place, so that when the Queen comes she will be deceived and will return to her own land." They gave the bird to the head of their officers, bidding him conceal her.

Asked he, "Where shall she be put?"

Marash replied, "There is no place so secret and secure as the prison that holds the robber." So the other carried the cage to the windowless dungeon, where Rasím lay grieving at his condition, and thrust it through the door, saying, "Here is a bird to keep thee company!" And at sight of him the nightingale began to sing so sweetly that the prison rats crept from their holes to hear.

As for Imer and Marash, they took a wild thrush and put it in a cage and hung it in the mosque and sent messengers to Queen Bôr to say for them, "Long life to Thy Majesty! Though we know not the purpose of thy coming, we give thee welcome as our royal guest."

In reply she sent them a letter, which said:

"And to you, Prince Imer and Prince Marash, long life! I come to take my nightingale Gizari from your mosque, and if ye do not surrender it, there shall be bloody war betwixt our armies."

To this they returned a soft answer, saying, "We know nothing of thy nightingale. It is true that a bird hangs in our mosque, but it is of little value, and if thou desirest it, it is our free gift to thee."

When she read this, Queen Bôr, with her chief officers, rode into the city and to the mosque, and looked at the wild bird in its cage, sitting silent. Said she to them, "This is not my Gizari. But I distrust these princes." And she bade her army encamp outside the city walls while she herself entered the palace as guest of Prince Imer and Prince Marash, who feasted and entertained her for seven days.

One evening she said to them, "By your leave I will ride with my officers about your city, that its sights may divert me For this is the hour when my lost nightingale was used to sing most sweetly, and I am most lonely."

They answered, "We will go with thee," and called for their horses and all set out together. So they rode through the parks and bazaars, till they chanced to skirt the wall of the prison, and suddenly she stopped her horse, and said she, "I hear somewhere a bird singing." Said Imer, "This is the city's prison and no bird can be in it." But she bade all listen and lo, muffled by the walls, the song of the nightingale in the windowless dungeon came to them.

Said she to Imer, "Open the prison gate this instant!" And, trembling, he gave the order. She straightway entered, and bade her officers search, till guided by the song, they burst open the door of the dungeon where Rasím lay in chains, with the jeweled cage beside him and the nightingale singing on its perch.

When she saw that it was indeed her Gizari, she looked at the cowardly brothers with eyes that shot forth black fire, and Imer, stammering, said, "O Queen, it was not we who stole her, but this man. We knew not the bird was thine till thou camest with thy troops. Then we were ashamed that he should have brought this reproach upon us, and though he is our own younger brother, we had him dragged here."

Asked she of Marash, "Is this true?"

He answered, "Yes. We waited only thy departure to have him hanged, after which we should have sent the bird to thee in thine own land."

She read the lie in their cowardly faces, and said she to her officers, "Take both of them to our camp and hold them there." And when they had gone out she asked Rasím, "Didst thou indeed steal my nightingale?"

He replied, "I am guilty before thee! I had built a

mosque to the glory of God, and I desired her singing to make it perfect."

"In the light of thy purpose," she said, "the deed could be forgiven thee. But I well know thou didst not steal her with thine own hand. Wert thou, indeed, in my garden?"

He answered, "Yes. I climbed its wall while thou wert asleep, not once, but twice. But each time at the sight of thy face my heart failed me."

At his words she knew he had fallen in love with her, and her heart beat as it had done when she had awakened on those two evenings. She suddenly remembered the rest of her dream which she had forgotten, and said she, "What didst thou do when thy heart failed thee? Tell me, that I may know thou art not a liar like thy brothers."

He replied, "I kissed thee."

Said she, "Do it again! But beware, for I have sworn that he who kisses me three times shall be my husband."

Then, in joy, he embraced her, and they kissed each other in love, and he told her all his story. And afterward she led her army into the city and took possession of it, and three days later Rasím and she were married, the festival lasting a whole month.

All their lives they lived in happiness together, with the nightingale Gizari to sing to them both, spending one year in his capital and one in hers. As for his brothers, Imer and Marash, they were sent into exile, and Imer went back to his barber shop and Marash to his coffee stall, and neither was ever heard of again.

They are there and here are we.
Just a tale for me and thee.

Acknowledgment

THE AUTHOR AND PUBLISHER wish to make acknowledgment of their indebtedness to the following publishers:

American Book Company for permission to use "The Phantom Cats" from *Japanese Folk and Fairy Tales* by Mary Nixon-Roulet, copyright 1908, 1937.

Doubleday & Company for permission to use "The Turquoise Princess" from *The Magic Bird of Chomo Lung Ma* by Sybille Noel, copyright 1931; and, "The Boy Who Stole the Nightingale That Was Called Gizari" from *Albanian Wonder Tales* by Post Wheeler, copyright 1936.

E. P. Dutton & Co., Inc., for permission to use "Shen of the Sea" from *Shen of the Sea* by Arthur Chrisman, copyright 1925.

Harcourt, Brace & Co., Inc., for permission to use "The Dragon's Strength" from *The Laughing Prince* by Parker Fillmore, copyright 1921.

Harper & Brothers for permission to use "Woman's Wit" from *Twilight Land* by Howard Pyle, copyright 1921.

Henry Holt & Company for permission to use "Story of Ali Baba and the Forty Thieves" from *The Arabian Nights* by Frances J. Olcott, copyright 1913, 1940.

Longmans, Green & Co., Inc. for permission to use "Three Fridays" from *Once the Hodja* by Alice G. Kelsey, copyright 1943; "Aladdin and the Wonderful Lamp" from *The Blue Fairy Book* by Andrew Lang, copyright 1929; and "The Story of the Seven Simons" from *The Crimson Fairy Book* by Andrew Lang, copyright 1903, 1931.

The Macmillan Company for permission to use "Sir Buzz" and "Valiant Vicky, the Brave Weaver" from *Tales of the Punjab*, copyright 1923 by Macmillan and Co. Ltd.